TIME FOR CHANGE

Volume II

Sequel to No Time Limit

By

J. MICHAEL O'CONNOR

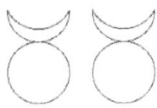

Other books by the author:

Ghosts of my Mind

His War, His Honor (a simple teacher)

No Time Limit

Fate

Volume Two (Time for Change) is dedicated to my beloved family.

A special thanks to Mrs. Sharon Clevinger for starting me on this authorship.

Art design by:

J. Michael O'Connor.

A special thank you to Melissa J. for her assistance.

All names, characters, and incidents portrayed in this novel are fictional. Therefore, no identification with or similarity to actual persons, living or dead, or actual events is intended or inferred.

ISBN: 978-1-959700-06-7

J. Michael O'Connor

[3]

J. Michael O'Connor

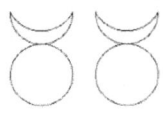

[5]

Narrator

The saga of a simple teacher. One that was not so simple. His life, his family, and all the individual lives which he touched were not in vain. Wherever James P. O'Francis is, I would like to tell him what an impact he had on many of his young minds. I found his passion for passing on knowledge to his students was legendary throughout the community.

However, there is always a negative with all the positives he created. The establishment could not and would not accept his unorthodox manner of delivering knowledge to his students. He would not "come in line." He was a free thinker. One that could not be put in a box. One that would not adhere to a cult-minded ideology. In time, their relentless assault on his character would be the opening of Pandora's Box. The haters of such an unusual teacher would reap the seeds they had sown. It was just a matter of *time*. The not-so-simple teacher once told me, "Peace of one's mind comes from the death of the wicked and evil."

Open-Wheeled Cars

It was May, and Jim's attention turned from umpiring baseball to auto racing. He had been in love with the "Indy" car and the Grand Prix cars from the time he first heard their high-pitched sound on the radio, thanks to his mother, who listened to the Indy race every year that he could remember.

Before he met Dawn, he went to a professional race-driving school to earn the right to drive open-wheeled race cars, F-1. He knew that the odds of becoming a professional race driver were even greater than that of a baseball player. But Jim had a skill that allowed him to at least be tested. He had demonstrated that with great success. Then he met Dawn, and it changed the course of his life forever. Maybe it was his fate?

His passion for the open-wheeled car and the beautiful sound of the high-pitched whine they produced stirred his blood every year. His Sundays were devoted to watching any Grand Prix race on TV, especially the famous Indianapolis 500. He never missed watching a race in its entirety, as he often wondered as he sat and watched a race, be it "Indy" or a GP race at some location in the world, which he preferred. What would have happened if he had not met Dawn? Would he have made it as an F-1 driver? Could he have met the enormous challenge of being such a superb athlete? It took skill to drive a race car at 200 miles an hour around a track, not to bump and touch your opponent, as did NASCAR's famous Southern auto sport.

Most people could not imagine in their wildest dreams what it was like. Jim had. In one brief moment in his life, he had experienced the thrill of driving a road course.

He was shifting gears at the flick of one's wrist, working one's feet from clutch to accelerator a multitude of times in a distance of a three-mile course, where the turning of the steering wheel could be measured in centimeters and directing the race car. The drivers would place their hands on the steering wheel at the "ten o'clock and the two o'clock" positions. They would be sitting in an open-wheeled car inches from the ground, practically lying down, obtaining speeds that could not be explained in words. In many ways, he was very envious of the drivers he would sit and watch as they skillfully drove the road courses of the world. The skills it took to make 500 miles on the most famous race track in the world at speeds that could not be felt by the millions that watched on television and the hundreds of thousands that descended on Indianapolis each year. Yet, on the other hand, the sheer terror engulfed his entire body when one of the cars lost control quicker than blinking one's eye, hitting a wall or a guard rail, or getting entangled.

There was no room for error in the world of the Grand Prix racers. Only someone who had at least been in one and experienced losing one could understand. James Patrick had been there and done that.

He would never forget the Sunday when it had rained all morning, and the student drivers had been in a classroom listening to a lecture by one of the professional driving instructors. He was young, daring, and full of life. He had made it home from an unpopular war and wanted more from whatever "it" was "out there." He wanted to experience it all, whatever fate had in his path. He wanted to reach out and grab hold of it and embrace it.

"Sir," another student raised his hand. "What do Grand Prix drivers do when it rains? Do they do like the "Indy" racers, or do they deal with it?"

Then, the instructor asked him his name, proudly stating it to him.

"They drive in it, no matter what. So the race goes on."

Jim waited for a few minutes and then raised his hand.

"Sir, are we going to drive today, as it is raining?"

The instructor smiled.

"Yes, we are, and in about ten minutes, we will see what kind of drivers you think you are."

He stepped to another instructor and asked him to get Jim's file. In a few minutes, he returned with it. As he opened it, he addressed James Patrick.

"I see here, Mr. O'Francis, you have done very well to this point. There is only one other person ahead of you in the class standings. I also see that you are in second place because you were caught speed shifting as you came out of the last set of "S's" onto the back straight away." He looked up at O'Francis.

Jim sat in his seat, saying nothing for a few moments. "Yes, sir, that is correct."

"You over-revved your engine in doing so. But, unfortunately for you, the red tachometer needle locked on how far your engine revved. If that had been one of the hundred-thousand-dollar machines you hope to drive one day, you could have lost an engine. That would have cost the owner a lot of money. And take you out of a race worth lots of money and points toward a world title."

Jim thought before he answered.

"Yes, but sir, I hope that by the time I am driving a car for someone that comes with that kind of price tag, I will have gained enough experience that this kind of mistake will not occur."

After finishing his lesson, the instructor just smiled and released the students to go to the track.

Unfortunately, the day did not go well for James Patrick as they did begin their training in drizzling rain. He was on his last lap of a timed ten-lap series, pushing his F-2 car to what he thought was its limits, when he came out of a double set of "S" turns onto a slopped back straight away of the famous Michigan International Speedway. Shifting to fifth gear, pressing his accelerator down hard, the back of his formula II race car gave to his left. He flinched his steering wheel to his left, as he was instructed to do, and the rear would fishtail a little and straighten up on a dry road, but not on a wet one. Instead, it sent him spinning in circles at over one hundred and ten miles an hour through the hay bales into the steel guardrail at the top of the oval backstretch.

The fiberglass surrounding the metal tube frame went into a thousand pieces, rupturing the water line running along the left side of the inside of the framing going from the small radiator to the engine, covering Jim in hot water. Other than being embarrassed and a little red from the hot water, he was unhurt.

After reviewing what he had done wrong and a good ass-chewing from several instructors, he learned a lesson he would long remember. He did not end up at the top of the class but did maintain his second-place position as he did have the skills it took to outdrive all the other drivers in his class, even the number one driver in the class, as was proven in a head-to-head race between the top five drivers in the class.

However, James Patrick's "Master" had other plans for him. His fate lay in another direction, and he had little to say about it.

Nevertheless, his passion for the Grand Prix race car remained strong as his blood and adrenaline raised every time he sat and watched the cars work their way through the turns and straightaways of the many worldwide courses, totally absorbed in each turn and pass of one of the most beautiful "whining" machines on earth.

8

Jim's summer was devoted to working around his home, seeing his psychoanalyst weekly, and being called to Holly's office several times to review material for the court case. The one thing he liked about her was that she was all business. She never contacted him to come to her office for meaningless conversations. Instead, he would spend no less than an hour each time they met.

He would spend his spare time researching how the law worked in a civil suit. He did not intend to make any mistakes. He viewed the case as a military war game. His life was at the very essence of this new battle, and he did not intend to lose. He took long walks in the hills surrounding his home to be close to nature and engulfed in the forest to keep himself mentally fit. He kept his physical body fit through his daily workouts in martial arts. In reality, he was honing his skills against his imaginary opponents and enemies.

David "Country" Higgenbottom would call from time to time, reviewing the changes of his military career, and seeking advice as to his next move, whether it was good or not. David had come into the O'Francis life as a youth and had been a constant presence. Jim and Dawn had become extremely close to Dave, the street boy Simms had kicked out of school, the English teacher who had fucked over him as a senior because he was not one of the higher social and economic students. His social background had been an albatross around his neck, but Jim had installed in him a will and a desire that he could achieve anything in life, no matter what the odds were. David received his high school equivalence degree and picked up his college courses whenever possible, at whatever military base. He received his military police degree and was named regimental soldier of the month twice. He had been awarded every peacetime ribbon that could have been given to him. He became a model soldier for the United States Army. But this call was slightly different; he had to decide if he should re-enlist for another four years.

If he did, the Army was sending him to Korea for 18 months. He had served eight at present and was due another promotion, another stripe, three up and two down. He had all the time in grade he needed and the required points in the now modern-day Army. A new type of evaluation that measured soldiers for them to get promoted.

Dave had grown up around the O'Francis home, where a person's word meant something. Jim reminded David that his words were all he owned. Whatever he told them, it measured his character. You say it; you own it.

John F. O'Donovan

I have followed James Patrick O'Francis and his saga for several years. I have done extensive research into his stories and events and found him to be of the utmost integrity.

I have, over the years, asked O'Francis to come to my place on the mountain to verify some information I had obtained.

An event that had occurred and that involved O'Francis. I needed verification.

I also left an "open door" policy to drop in whenever he needed to escape the rest of the "world."

I lived in a semi-remote area some distance from Reynolds County, where I bought up all the land surrounding my home keeping most of the world's people away.

I was a freelance writer for many years and traveled a good part of the world to cover many different stories. I had been very successful and semi-retired to the mountains of the easternmost part of Tennessee on the western border of North Carolina.

I had not intended to do any significant writing and enjoy my time away from the triumphs and tragedies of people and their daily lives.

For whatever reason, I was attracted to O'Francis and his life. So I began writing again, not just the short stories for a major magazine or "by-line" for some newspaper. I decided to write a book. A book on a world that I had little knowledge of. I felt that most people in the United States knew little about education systems.

I was researching and learning about the real world of education. But, locked behind the many thousands of schools throughout the nation, locked behind the brick walls throughout the country, I concentrated primarily on the ones in Reynolds County. I found not what I had expected, nor was it what most people of most cities, towns, and communities would have expected.

I noticed that the most information one might get about the public education system was an occasional headline story on national news networks.

I became burnt out with traveling, asking questions, and seeing the horror and depression of many different races, ethnic groups, and genders of people. However, for whatever reason, O'Francis' life was different. I was inspired by the life O'Francis led, and once again, I began to write with great enthusiasm. I am John F. O'Donovan, and I am continuing with the O'Francis story.

Jim arrived at my home at 10:00 A.M., in his language, 1000 hours. He just needed a place to get away for a while. So we had a few cups of coffee and some small talk, and then he went into one of his silent modes for a good thirty minutes as he looked out from the back deck into the woods surrounding my home.

"You know, John, what I was just thinking about, for whatever reason?"

I got up from my chair, walked to his side, and leaned over on the rail with him. "No, what?"

He giggled, rose, stretched his back and upper shoulders, took a drink of his coffee, and asked for a refill. Then, he returned and continued his story.

"Do you remember me telling you about the incident with Damon Bales and Richard Finkel over the son of bitch thing?"

"Yes, I do."

"Well, I had something like that happen to me long ago. Would you like to hear about it? It has been on my mind, and I wanted to tell you. Oh, guess you had better get your recorder."

So I went into the house, retrieved it from my desk, checked the batteries, removed the tape where I had taped him several months earlier, replaced it with a blank one, and quickly returned.

"Okay, I am ready."

Jim giggled again and began with a big smile on his face.

"The Bales ordeal reminds me of an incident when I was getting ready to ship out for Nam. We were working on a dock loading and moving shit, something to keep us troops busy. That was the Army's way, you know. We were in San Francisco, and I was acting stupid, as were others. Garbassing around. Shit, just having fun, like young boys will. I should say, young men, you know, just really killing time. Shit, I was only twenty-one years old. It was the first time I had not been in some training since I had been in the service. Hell, I knew where we were going, did not know what the hell was facing me, but at any rate, we were fucking around, and this hard-ass sergeant, who had joined us at the port, was in charge of the "laborers." I did not know him and had not seen him before, but he was in charge of us.

"Well, he started barking orders at us, being all serious. Several of us, as well as myself, took him and his orders lightly and started laughing. We got the giggles, and it did not make any difference what one of us did or said, or for that matter, what he said. We laughed. Well, he got pissed, decided to exercise his authority, and broke badass. Hell, we were not laughing at him. Really, we were laughing at ourselves and the entire situation. Well, at any rate, he picked on good ole me out of the six or eight that were having some fun and got in my face like we were in boot camp and were a new group of raw recruits like most DIs do.

Some things I noticed about people in uniforms: one, is if they have wings on their chest and two, if they have a Ranger tab on their left shoulder. He had none. In his zealous effort to show his authority with his E-6 rank, he called me a son of a bitch. At that time, being very young and on the somewhat arrogant side with a Ranger tab on my left shoulder and a set of silver wings on my chest, I got straight quickly. So, I was nose to nose with him and said...

Jim paused for a moment, took a drink of coffee, and cleared his throat.

"Now, let me interject here for a moment. My mother was more than just close. She raised me alone for the most part. She was my rock, my ear for listening, and my advisor. She had a tough life and worked many hours as a nurse. And she was really a good nurse. Over the years, after returning to this part of the world, I have had many people tell me what a great nurse she was. We struggled financially, and she worked two jobs. Hospital and private nursing to make ends meet. I mean, I can go on and on about the heroics of my mother. The point here is she was not a bitch. And being young, I took the comment very personally. So as I was telling you...

"Look, Sarg, you can yell at me. You can get in my face. I can deal with that. But, DO NOT call my mother a bitch! You got that!

"Now, there ain't nobody laughing anymore. The point of fact is, one of the "laughing boys" stated, 'Oh shit, it is on now'...the middle-aged gung-ho sergeant took offense to my tone of voice. And given that I was only a corporal at the time and had stepped close enough to be literately nose-to-nose to the over-bearing Sergeant."

He replied quickly.

"Look, you so-called badass youngster," as he was looking at my left shoulder, "those god-damn tabs don't mean shit to me! Hell, anybody can get one of them...you sons a bitches ain't half what you are made out to be! I'll clean this fuck'en dock with all of you!"

"Soooo, my reaction was swift, no thought was put into what I did, and I took him out with one punch with my left fist under the middle of his right jaw. He hit the dock, and his eyes rolled back until the whites showed. I walked off and went up on the deck of the ship. Now keep in mind here, John, I knew after I had calmed down, which was in a matter of minutes, that I had fuckkkkked-up."

"Well, I did not know another Sergeant, one Gregory African, a Caucasian, an odd name I know, but he was an E-5 and had been close enough to see and hear the entire event. Oh yeah, by the way, he did have a set of wings on his chest. Later we became close, but that, too, is another story. Anyway, I had to report to the First Sergeant, and let me tell you, you really did not want to have to go to him in trouble. Hell, I did not want to go to him when I was not in trouble. God, he scared the hell out of me. Shit, he was about six-six and weighed ahh, shit, I guess two-forty or better, solid as a brick wall.

"He had a voice that sounded like God or what one would perceive as God's voice. You know, deep, powerful, commanding. The kind that you damn sure listened to when he spoke. The kind that when you were being "dressed down," you had goosebumps all over your body, and the temperature would be in the nineties. The hair on the back of your neck stood up like a dog's when he was about to meet a foe. I did not know Sergeant African had already given him a full incident report.

"Of course, Sergeant Powell, the man I decked, had filed charges against me. The First Sergeant chewed my ass out so bad that I had none when I left the office he had brought me into. Hell, I do not know if it was one of the Navy personnel's offices. I do not know what they call their offices and do not know anything about the Navy language. But, he had to do something with me. I mean, a corporal could not deck an E-6 and get away with it. So, he assigned me to pull KP for the entire trip, thirty-five days plus a stop-over in Subic-bay, Okinawa. All on the largest ocean on earth. Then another short trip to the tropical paradise of Viet Nam."

Jim took another drink of coffee.

"The day before we arrived in the country of Viet Nam, the First Sergeant called me back into the office, probably the Captain of the ship's office. Hell, I don't know. But he told me why he had to do what he did. Then he smiled and said he would have done the same thing. He was not pressing charges against me, an article 15, which would have cost me time and grade and most likely some jail time in Nam. Damn, just think, go to Viet Nam and go to jail. God, what a thought.

"But, he did commend me for my job on KP, which I did a good job. Hell, I just had fun doing what I had to do. I mean, John, where was I going? I was out at sea, and it was lots of fun seeing everyone get sick, puking in their food, and everywhere else. Shit, we went through some damn big ass storm, the ship's front, ahh, what the hell they call it? I do not know, anyway, it would go up, like forty-five degrees up, and then, smack. It would hit the water like it had just bottomed out. It jarred the hell out of you. Then just as soon as it hit, it came up again—Lord, what a ride and puking troops all over the ship.

"Before you ask, I did not get sick, not once, not even during the wild ride through the storm. I have no idea why. I just told myself that I would not get sick, and I did not."

Jim finished his cup of coffee and needed another refill. He was off to the kitchen; a few minutes later, he returned and had brought with him a black rectangular cigar container with four cigars in it.

"John, do you mind if I smoke a cigar out here."

Of course, I did not, so Jim pulled one out of his container, went through a cigar ritual, and lit it. He then picked up where he had left off.

"However, that has been on my mind for whatever reason, and I just wanted to tell you that little story. That is why I made much of a joke out of the SOB thing with Bales. I mean, we are not young now, and we have done and said the same thing over the years, to all kinds of people, in jest and being serious. John, we also mean you."

I looked at him, and he had a slight grin.

"Well, Jim, do you regret telling Finkel that Damon was a son of a bitch?"

"No, not really. I mean, I would like to think that his mother was not responsible for how he turned out. But I guess it was just a means of insulting him. Which I truly intended to do. And he deserved it. So no, I do not regret what happened in the sequence of events back then! However..."

He stopped talking, walked a few steps toward the far end of the deck, and turned back toward me. The smoke from his cigar trailed behind him.

"In hindsight and all that I have uncovered, I regret trying to get that damn trophy! Which did lead to the confrontation with Finkel, which led to Bales. But, I have come to realize that I was blinded by loyalty."

We talked about several other teachers in the system and how Marshy was treating them, and Jim enlightened me on some of the facts I did not have. Then he just up and left, leaving me with a pile of unanswered questions, which was not all that unusual for Jim. However, knowing him as I now do, he figured that I was the journalist, my story, and that I was the one to find the truth if that was what I was seeking.

Another Principal

James Patrick made many trips to his psychotherapies for over a year but was not better. His court case was going slow. Holly had difficulty getting material back from Damon's attorney in the allotted time. He appeared to be able to get an extension on some of the most trivial matters, which to Jim was legal bull shit, as he was beginning to learn about the legal profession firsthand. This made his mental condition worse as he began to feel bad about doing things by lawful means. Another doctor was called in, a psychologist named Celia Flora, hopefully to help Jim with his stress and what was identified as PTSD.

A new principal had arrived at Honsburg Middle, Mr. Scott Jackson Wolffe, and he was making inquiries concerning O'Francis. O'Francis did have some information concerning Mr. Wolffe but felt he needed to know more. So

Jim called and requested more info on S. J. Wolffe from "The Man." In a short time, Jim received information about Wolffe, delivered in a brown manila envelope by a young man Jim had seen several times when envelopes were delivered.

Mrs. Mazo was in her room working with her science class when Scott Wolffe called her out into the hallway to talk to her.

"Bernadette, you and I have been friends since high school, and I would like you to give me some information on Mr. O'Francis."

Bernadette had a cold chill run over her body at his request. She liked Jim, and they had been working together very well since his arrival. They had shared ideas that both had incorporated into their classroom.

O'Francis and Mazo expounded on several topics that most people avoided. Religion and science, politics, and the school system. The community and the self-righteous attitude that many people held. The community's so-called social elite looked upon certain people in and around the town. They found a common bond, adjusted to each other, agreed on some matters, disagreed, and remained good acquaintances and professional colleagues.

O'Francis found that she was a very open-minded person and listened to his point of view on various matters they seemed to find themselves conversing. She was intelligent and not easily fooled by other people and did not take what she heard as fact.

Jim often turned to her for advice on teaching on the middle school level and took her suggestions as they seemed to work. But unfortunately, he had never been trained to teach on the level he had been demoted to and often found himself struggling to reach the ten through thirteen-year-old students. Jim's expectations of students entering middle school prepared fall far short.

The earlier beginnings of doubt about Mrs. Mazo had faded to the foggy pits of his memory, and he chose to leave them there. His earlier suspicions that she had gone to Simms about their conversation proved unjust. All indications had pointed elsewhere. His little voice told him she was an ally and not an enemy or "spy" for the bastardized administrators that seemed to come and go like some revolving door operation. The how as to how Simms found out about their conversation was a file left open? However, he became convinced that Bernadette was not the one who took the conversation to Simms. He found that she had a great deal of integrity, spirit, and grit— something Jim had grown to admire in her.

The two had reached the point of real personal Q and A's.

O'Francis was working overtime. It was 1600 hours, and he was grading papers and getting some maps reorganized and in the order he wanted his students to work on.

He was standing at the back of the room when Bernadette Mazo walked in. Learning from word of mouth and her personal experience early in their professional relationship, you did not walk up behind him and announce yourself. And you never touched him from behind. Instead, she spoke softly as she stood just inside his classroom door.

"Jim, do you have a few minutes?"

As he turned, he answered, "Sure, what can I do for you?"

"Jim, I would like to ask you something, and I do not want you to get mad at me."

"Well, I do not know quite how to answer that, but as far as asking me a question, which by your opening is a rather, shall I say a heavy question."

"Well, it is, and I want to go to the person in which the rumor mill is still turning its wheels around. I feel as if you and I have reached a professional relationship where we can talk about personal topics without offending one another."

At that point in the conversation, Jim did not respond, as he felt that there were really some questions on her mind that were really bothering her, and she needed to get a direct answer from him.

"Okay with all this?" Bernadette continued, looking James P. directly in his eyes from some ten feet away as she had walked to the middle of the room. O'Francis's classroom desks were arranged in a U shape, and his desk was in the far corner of the room. His classroom setting was unlike 99% of all classrooms. Most, if not all, teachers had their desks in the center of the front of the room with desks in parallel rows.

Jim had a puzzled look on his face.

"If there is something on your mind, hell Bernadette, just ask. If I think it is too personal, I will tell you, and if it is something in which I can answer, I will. But, hell, there is one thing you can be damn sure of. You will get a straight answer. In addition, Bernadette, you just may not like what you hear. Now, is that fair enough for you?"

"Fair enough. Okay, did you ever have any relationships with your girl basketball players?"

James Patrick was not expecting that question, and it took him aback a moment.

"Well, well, that is a bit of a surprise. Wow, rumor mill, the same old shit is still gushing through the sewer line of the hallways of the school system. Okay, let's clear a few things up first. You used the word relationship. Let me clarify that first. The answer to that is yes. But purely fatherly, as an advisor, a counselor, and a coach. There was never, and I repeat, with resounding emphasis, no infidelity to my wife on my part. There was no fornicating between "my girls" and myself. I mean, damn, they were teenagers. Mature, yes, but by god, that kind of conduct is not in my wheelhouse! Now, Bernadette, that is a fact and what others in this lovely community and the school system would like to think; well, I cannot control that. The girls are now of the age that any one of them will tell you the truth to your face if asked. Unless anyone has changed, you will get a candid to your, face answer. But, I dare say none will deviate from what I have attested to. I had and have the utmost respect for all of them. My god, they were teenagers, for Christ's sake! Damn, I was fifteen years older than they were. These people who insist on tainting my character are mentally sick! And, Bernadette, most likely all good Christians!"

There was sternness and resentfulness in James Patrick's voice, which created a bit of uneasiness in the room. Then, finally, silence filled the classroom, and Bernadette just looked at Jim.

"You know Bernadette; this good loving, caring Christian community does not understand that I have some ethics. Unlike others which I have had to work with and around. You see, these people who continue to spread the filth about me and character assassinate me are the very ones that have no ethics whatsoever. And yes, Bernadette, it is called character assassination. There is not one damn thing a person can do about it. If you try to defend yourself publicly, you simply make matters worse. People will either believe what they are told via the many gossip grapevines, adding to whatever they may have heard. Then slander grows like cancer until it kills the character of the person it was intended to kill."

They stood facing one another across the classroom; not a word was spoken for two minutes.

Bernadette then broke a slight smile on her face.

"I did not think so. Thank you, Mr. O'Francis, for your candidness and your integrity." She turned and bounced her petite body out of the room.

When Jim talked to me concerning his daily teaching of the students and his problems of reaching the students at the age he was now forced to teach, he enlightened me to the fact that all "teachers" cannot just walk into a class and teach a subject. Nor can they teach any age group because they have the title of a "teacher." Nor, for that matter, a degree in whatever field they choose to enter the teaching profession. A master's or even beyond does not make you a good teacher.

After such a long time talking to Jim, I reflected on my college days and remembered that all professors were not good teachers. A Ph.D. did not make you a good teacher, and now I realize that it did not make good high school teachers or any other educational level.

Like most of the mass public, I really do not understand the innermost workings of any school system and that degrees in education tend to intimidate or impress most people on the street. But, at any rate, let me continue with my story...

Wolffe asked Mrs. Mazo, "Do you find him hard to get along with?"

"No, Scott, I don't. Why. Who said he was?"

"Well, Bernadette, I was told he gave Simms a hard time. That none of you got along with him. That he had an attitude toward you."

"Well, I don't know who you have been talking to. All that you have said is not true."

Scott made the mistake of asking Bernadette, "Are you sure?"

At that, she became irritated with Wolffe's insinuation.

"Look, Mr. Wolffe. I don't know what you want me to say, but I will not tell you what you want to hear. You asked me, and I told you. Now, if you want to get someone else to tell you what you would like to hear, I suggest that you go get your information from someone else!"

She then turned and went back to her class.

That same day, Scott Wolffe met Mr. O'Francis ascending the stairs at the furthermost end of the school building and headed toward his classroom.

"Hello, Mr. O'Francis. How are things going so far this year?"

Jim continued to walk down the stairs to the first landing, then paused. He could detect a devious tone in his voice. The two men stood at the top of the last flight of stairs leading to the first-floor hallway, and directly across the stairs was Jim's classroom.

"Mr. Wolffe, I have never worked for you, and I think you and I should get off on the right foot. So let me say, you just come clean with me, and I will answer any questions you might have. It will most likely save you a lot of work trying to get the information from other people who do not know me."

James Patrick's candidness caught Wolffe off guard, and he exposed himself for a brief moment with a quick curt response.

"Well, I know you don't like administrators, but," and before he could finish, O'Francis interrupted.

"You know! How do you know that? I have never worked for you. So why would you group all administrators into one category? Unless all of **YOU** are the same. Now, Mr.

Wolffe, you are correct if that is the case. I do not like any administrator, starting with your Führer!"

At that, Scott Wolffe looked at James P. with a puzzled face, and O'Francis knew he had tripped him with the word Führer in an instant.

"Mr. Wolffe, I am referring to the superintendent, your leader. The man you follow so loyally, pledging allegiance to!"

"Now, wait a minute. I am not like all the rest of these principals in the county. I do not agree with every little thing that Mr. Marshy does."

Jim was quick with a response. "And I do not place ALL administrators in the same group! Point of fact is, Mr. Wolffe, I have worked for a couple of outstanding, honest, and honorable principals since I have been working for Reynolds County." Then there was a short pause in their conversation. Jim never took his eyes off Mr. Wolffe.

"And, Mr. Wolffe, let me add, I have worked for some of the evilest, malicious, mendacious, and corrupt principals in this or any other county in Virginia!"

Wolffe stood looking at O'Francis for just a moment and then lost eye contact and began looking from the floor to the walls or down the stairs, but not at O'Francis.

Jim, spoke with anger in his voice.

"But I will bet my "pissey" ass little paycheck against yours that you will do precisely what your Fuhrer tells you to do. And I will bet it will be done without questioning him!"

"Do what?" Scott stated.

"I am referring to your statement about not agreeing with your Fuhrer."

"I think you are wrong in feeling that way, Mr. O'Francis. I am here to help you in any way I can. I just want you to know that. I mean, I am not like Damon Bales. I think you have been done a terrible wrong."

O'Francis retaliated with a sarcastic tone.

"Well, I thank you for your deep concern, Mr. Wolffe. However, I have one question for you. Just where did you get the idea that I hated all administrators?"

O'Francis emphasized all administrators in a tone that left no doubt of what he meant.

"I mean, you cannot personally attest to that, as you and I have never worked with each other. And just in case you may have missed that, I want to repeat myself for you to understand me and the working together. Not me, just working for you in this school. So, Mr. Wolffe, just why would you make such a sweeping generalized statement to me like that?"

At the end of James P.'s stunning statement, Scott Wolffe began a nervous shifting of the feet and hands and started walking down the stairs without responding to O'Francis' question. O'Francis walked a step behind his new principal. Finally, they reached the first-floor hallway and walked the short fifteen feet to Jim's classroom door.

"Well, Mr. O'Francis, I hope you and I can work together this year, and if there is anything you might need, just come and ask."

"Mr. Wolffe, I surmise each of you administrators rehearses that at the beginning of each year as you pledge allegiance to your Fuhrer! So I bid you a good day, sir!"

Scott Wolffe then turned and headed off down the hall quickly. Jim stood and watched him and smiled to himself.

The bell rang, and the students filled the hallway. Wolffe became engulfed in the masses of students as they went to and fro to their next class. Finally, as his last student entered his famous "Think Tank," he spoke softly to himself, "Shitttttttttt!"

Scott Wolffe's notorious reputation for sexual activity with his teachers continued at Honsburg Middle School. The

35-year-old Pat Cuffel Special Ed teacher provided him with all he wanted on and off school grounds.

The local political machine had appointed Robert Studer to the School Board to support LaMar. LaMar made Robert's brother John the new principal of Liberty High.

Before Hobbit, Manual's principal left for a more honorable working environment. He had placed Emmanuel on a steering committee as the chairperson for the school's self-study, and taking his assignment seriously, he had been doing an outstanding job.

But LaMar felt that he had too much power and instructed Norberta, the new principal of Elk Horn Elementary school and another of Marshy's part-time mistresses, to remove him as the chairperson.

Emmanuel had also been appointed to the technical committee and worked with the people in Richmond to establish a future for tech labs in Reynolds County.

He was also appointed part of a visiting team for school renewal in another county. All that came to an abrupt stop the first week that Norberta Millicent arrived as the principal of Elk Horn School.

Emmanuel left his new principal's office, reeling from the verbal insulting attack from his new principal for what appeared to be no apparent reason Manual was removed from all committees he had been previously assigned. The loyal lieutenants were performing their duties as instructed.

The Path Forks

James Patrick O'Francis arrived at Chicago's O'Hare from a flight out of Atlanta. He had been provided with four different identifications to travel from Montana to Atlanta.

His trip would begin in Helena, Montana, as Timothy S. Daly. That would take him to Phoenix, Arizona. Next, he would be William Matt Molly as he traveled to Houston, Texas. In Houston, he would present his ticket at the counter as John W. Kilpatrick and travel to Atlanta, Georgia. None of the flights were connecting. It would appear that all originated from one origin. It took a full day and several hours for James P. to make his trip, but he did not object and fully understood what Paul had done. When Jim arrived in Chicago, he felt secure that if a check were done as to where he had traveled from, it would be Atlanta, Georgia.

Joseph checked the flight from Atlanta to determine if it was on time. A mere fifteen minutes late, not bad, so he headed off to O'Brien's Restaurant and Bar, where Jim had been instructed to meet Joseph and Michael close to Terminal 3, where he was to arrive.

Thirty-five minutes later, James P. entered O'Brien's Pub. He scanned the room. He saw Joseph and Michael sitting at a table toward the back of the room. Michael spotted Jim first and could see him scanning the room, and he directed his attention toward them. As the two men rose, Joseph tossed a twenty-dollar bill on the table and walked toward O'Francis. With big smiles on their faces, they greeted each other.

"Afternoon, Jim."

"Afternoon, Joseph, Michael." Michael then reached for Jim's garment bag.

"May I take that?"

"Sure. Thanks, Michael." They then walked to the parking lot and headed for the Northside of Chicago.

Arriving at the Caprotti home, Jim was shown to a guest room, more like someone's master bedroom. Afterward, Maria gave him the grand tour while Joseph was on the phone with his father-in-law.

Nina Maria was the proud daughter of a powerful executive who also happened to be the head of a "Family." Her five foot two inches small framed body was shaped like an hourglass, with a firm 36-inch breast line, a 24-inch waist, and a mere one hundred and ten pounds. She had short dark brown hair with a naturally dark complexion. She had no children and looked ten years younger than her forty-nine years. She had been educated in a private school and received her higher education from her father's alumni, De Paul. She majored in international business and worked for her father. She had become known in the business circles as a cold, hard-driving corporate executive. Her father was incredibly proud of her.

Joseph found them in the back of the house, touring the pool, the pool house, the sauna, and Jacuzzi.

"So, Jim ole friend, what do you think?" Joseph asked as he joined them in entering the pool house, which had its wet bar, small bedroom (10x12), apartment size kitchen, and one bath.

"Well, Joseph, my man, I think you have done very well for yourself, very well indeed." O'Francis had a little giggle, smiling at Joseph. Joseph asked, "What?"

"Well, this is better than the pool halls and bars you and I once adorned."

"Joseph laughed; yea, sure is. Jim, we are joining Maria's father for dinner. Do you need to shower?"

"Yes, I would like to. Is this a formal gathering?"

"No, no, no, this is a jeans gathering." Both Maria and Joseph laughed, knowing that Jim was not quite at ease and did not know what to expect from Vincent Spadalini. It was up to them to make him feel at ease at the Caprotti house and the Spadalini home.

As they approached the double iron gates of the Spadolini estate, Joseph pushed the button on the box attached to the post ten feet or so from the gates. From the box, a voice asked. "May I help you?"

"Tony, its Joseph." The gates opened, and they proceeded. A camera began tracking them into the estate, and the gates closed behind them. Another two hundred yards of the concrete driveway to a thirty-yard squared open area in front of the main house. Maria went into the house first.

"Momma, Dad, we're here," she called out as she entered the large foyer.

The large home in Don Spadalini's homeland would have been called a villa. The odor of an Italian dinner permeated the lower level of the Spadalini mansion. Maria knew just where she would find her mother. She went straight to the kitchen. There was no real need for Sophia Nina Spadalini to be in the kitchen, but her love for cooking was a hobby, and she would have to be considered an expert at it, as their chef would often tell her.

As James P. would learn about her hobby, his thoughts were that Dawn and Sophia would have gotten along very well. However, the death of Dawn still left a deep void in Jim's soul even after many years had passed.

Maria was a clone of her mother, just that Sophia was older with black hair with no graying even at the age of 65 and looked as if she had never had a child.

The Spadalini residence was kept immaculately clean, with an entire staff of maids and groundskeepers. On a typical day, a cooking staff fixed all the meals unless Sophia wanted her hand in cooking, despite her social prominence and the gala events she attended with Vincent, pressing the flesh with local and national political figures—often including corporate tycoons.

However, this dinner was not typical, and Sophia helped direct the meal for a special guest, a trusted friend of Joseph's. Someone who had been in the right place at the right time to ensure that he lived a long life and wed to the daughter of a Don. To Vincent and Sophia, that made O'Francis special.

James P. did not feel special. The point of fact was he felt a bit out of place. He was in the presence of an influential figure and an extremely wealthy man that controlled a large corporation with ties in powerful places. Not just in the

Illinois government but in the Nation's Capitol. James P. was not easily intimidated by anyone, but in this case, he felt a bit intimidated by Don Vincent Spadalini, even though Vincent did not blatantly display intimidation. He was very cordial. It was the fact that O'Francis was very aware of his position and power.

Vincent was a handsome man standing six foot two, well-trimmed, one hundred and ninety pounds, salt and pepper short well-groomed hair, and clean shaven. His voice was not very deep, medium, and a slightly Italian accent. He did not look as if he was 68 years old.

Senators, congresspersons, attorneys, and judges never got him uptight, even though they too had power in many places. They liked to wield that power and make people feel intimidated by their position, power, and stature. Those types of people did not bother O'Francis. He more or less brushed them off, like lint on his suit coat. However, this man, Vincent Spadalini, was different. He had an air about him. His posture and walk commanded great respect without words or boastfulness of titles or positions. When he spoke, it reminded Jim of the E. F. Hutton commercial. Everyone listened. James P. quickly analyzed Mr. Spadalini. He appeared to Jim to be a low-key person, not one to get overly excited, very analytical, and rarely raised his voice.

The dining area was quite large, a 30x40 foot room with a large dining table in the middle. It looked as if it had been handmade, and upon inquiring, he found that the table was handmade and shipped from Sicily, a family heirloom dating back to Vincent's great grandfather. Jim admired the room, commenting on the decor. O'Francis could see the pride on Sophie's face as he commented on her dining room and the pride in the table as Vincent went into detail about the history of a magnificent piece of woodwork.

The family gathered around the table, and James P. was given a place directly across from Don Spadalini. *Odd,* his thoughts flashed through his mind, *the Don sitting in the middle with his wife to his left.* To Jim's right was Maria and to his left Joseph. Jim had not expected that type of dining arrangement. Sophia instructed everyone that grace was to be said to add to the unexpected seating arrangements, and all bowed their heads. "Bless us O Lord...." the well-known and traditional Catholic dinner prayer, of which James P. recited along with the rest of the Spadalini family, "through Christ our Lord..." and a slight pause, and Vincent ended with the Amen. Something Jim could tell was done each time they were together.

Sophia looked across at Jim, "You are Catholic, I take it?" A slight smile was on her face.

"Yes, I am. In a way. One might say, a recovering one." He continued. "Being Irish, with my ancestral heritage from the County Tipperary, and being the third generation of my family here in the United States." No one commented on the part of his statement, "recovering."

At that point, the maid brought in the dinner and began placing the food on the table. Vincent opened a bottle of wine and offered his guest the first glass. There was lots of wine at the meal, and several bottles were consumed before the meal was over.

After Jim took a long drink of wine, Don Spadalini asked, "So what do you think of the wine?"

"Well, I am not a wine connoisseur, but I like it. But, of course, I am Irish, and you know what they say about us Irish and alcohol."

All had a good laugh. As the meal proceeded, the conversation was light, with a joke thrown in occasionally with lots of laughter. Then, as all were about to finish their meal, the conversation turned a little more serious as Don Spadalini asked, "Jim, do you know a Brian Keefe O'Francis?"

Jim thought for a few seconds. "No, sir, I do not think so." There was yet another short pause in the conversation.

"Do you have a brother?" Jim looked at Vincent Spadalini.

"No, sir, I am the only son from my father's loins." Then with a bit of a laugh, he added, "I might add, to my knowledge, and that too is somewhat of a long story— my father that is. Why do you ask?"

There was a rather long pause in the conversation from Vincent as he took the last bit of his veal and then a sip of wine to finish his meal. Then, for the second time during the meal, there was silence as James P. finished his wine, and Sophia asked if he would like more, and O'Francis extended his glass across the table for her to fill his glass. Then Vincent reached his glass to his wife for her to fill his.

"Because I do some business with Mr. O'Francis, and he could be your brother, looks that is. Where did you say you were from?"

"Well, I was born in Oklahoma. But I was raised in the southern part of Virginia with my grandparents and mother."

Yet another long pause occurred again in the conversation, and with some degree of hesitation, James P. continued.

"My mother and father separated when I was very young. So I never got to know my father. I was only three when they separated."

In her Italian accent, Sophia spoke, "Ooooh, that is not good. Family is important. A son needs his father when he is growing up. Did you not go look for him?"

As Jim answered, Don Spadalini spoke, "Enough of that. How about some dessert?"

"Sure, I think I can handle a little."

For dessert, they had spumoni ice cream. As the maid brought the dessert out, Sophia asked Jim if he had ever had spumoni ice cream.

"Yes, Mrs. Spadalini, I have and quite often. My mother-in-law was Italian, and I am very acquainted with spumoni ice cream."

James P. and Sophie began a much lighter conversation between them.

"Where was she from?"

Jim was in the process of taking a small bite and took a moment to answer.

"Her roots are in Palermo, Sicily."

A big smile came across her face. "My grandparents are from Palermo."

Sophia and Jim continued a conversation about her family, and no one else did any talking during the next ten-minutes. Then Maria joined in on the conversation.

"Where do you live now, Jim?" A moment passed, and Joseph turned and looked at Maria *as if to say*, do not ask that question. Joseph then looked at his father-in-law, all in two seconds. Coffee had been served with the spumoni ice cream, and Jim had started to drink from his cup. And he slowly finished before answering Maria's question.

He then gently placed the elegant coffee cup onto the saucer and, without any wavering, answered, "I live just north of Atlanta, Georgia. I have a home in the very southern tip of the Appalachian Mountains."

"I always thought that Georgia was flat," Maria stated.

James P. smiled as the moment of tension with Joseph seemed to pass with each answer Jim gave to Maria.

"Well, Maria, most of the state is. However, the long two thousand mile Appalachian mountain ranges end in the northernmost part of the state. I found a place between Atlanta and Chattanooga, Tennessee, along the North Carolina border that suited me, and I retired there. The winters are not bad, and yet you have your four seasons. Summers can get a little hot, but I am not far from the Great Smoky Mountains, and the air in the mountains is often ten degrees cooler than it is in the flat areas or the cities surrounding the area."

"I hear that the Smoky Mountains are real nice."

Jim smiled. "Yes, they are, and it is a real nice place to visit. I think you would enjoy the area."

He looked over at Joseph.

"I think Joseph should take you there for a week's vacation and get some good clean southern mountain air in your lungs."

Joseph just smiled and took a drink of his coffee.

Q and A Time

After dinner, Vincent took James P. on a tour of his estate. Vincent appeared to enjoy describing the house in great detail, ending up in the back garden, where a bottle of Glenfiddich Scotch, two glasses, a bucket of ice, and a box of Montecristo, 50 rings, six inch long cigars had been placed on the table in the gazebo.

"I understand that you like scotch or Irish whiskey."

"Yes, sir, I do like both." Vincent proceeded to open the bottle and fill both glasses.

"With two cubes of ice, correct?"

Jim just smiled and replied softly, "Yes."

"I am told you like a good cigar with your after-dinner drink."

Again a smile crossed O'Francis's face. "Yes, I do."

Vincent reached over and opened the humidor. "Get yourself one."

He pointed to the lighter and the cutter, then clipped the end off and lit his cigar. Don Spadalini did the same and, with the glass of scotch in his hand, turned and faced O'Francis.

"I salute you." His statement took Jim by complete surprise. Vincent read his face.

"You ask yourself why I should salute you." Jim could not speak. He just nodded his head yes.

"I will tell you. Would you like to walk while we talk, or would you rather sit?"

"Walk," O'Francis replied.

"Good. I also like to walk while I talk." Then, with his glass of scotch in his right hand, Vincent indicated for Jim to walk the vast back garden, an area of at least three acres of exceptionally well-cared-for lawns, shrubs, trees, and flowers.

"Why do I salute you, you ask? Because all these years, you have never, not once, asked anything in return for what you did for Joseph. I would not have Joseph, whom I consider a son, without you. My daughter was deeply in love with him and, as you know, married him. She would not be happily married if it were not for you."

James P. said nothing and just walked alongside Vincent.

"I know that you knew that you could have asked for anything you wanted. I know this. Most people would have asked for something. I would have given it to them. But you went on with your own life, leaving the area without a word—

no requests, no favors, nothing. You are a man with honor. I like men with honor. I know you can be trusted. I know you are a man of your word. I know these things. It is my business to know people. Especially people I want to get to know. Joseph has enlightened me about some of your hardships, yet you ask for nothing, even with his offer to help you. Why? He owes you his very life. Now, why do I ask you?"

It was time for a re-fill as they had taken a short walk and approached the gazebo. Jim was still somewhat nervous inside, even with the wine he had consumed throughout the hour or so with dinner and a double shot of scotch. His outward appearance showed a calm, ice-cold approach to a man in a position of power he really could not relate to. Yet here he was talking to Jim as if he was of an equal statue, talking carefree as if he had known him for a long time. James P. did not understand and was not yet at ease with the "Don" of the Spadalini Family.

"Don Spadalini." Vincent Spadalini interrupted Jim. "It is just Vincent, Jim, okay?"

"Yes, sir," Jim replied with respect to a gentleman a mere three years his senior. Then he continued.

"I do not know how to answer your question. I did not feel that Joseph owed me anything. When I learned of his connections to you, I still did not feel you, nor did Joseph, owe me anything. I did what I had to do at the time, and that was it. As you know, he and I became very well acquainted, and I liked Joseph. But I..."

Then a long pause, a drink, a few puffs. Jim's insides quivered ever so slightly.

"I... I... do not like getting really close to people. Friends, that is. I..." Another pause, as the two men began to walk again, Vincent said nothing, letting Jim explain.

"I lost several very close friends a long time ago... I have never gotten over it. I did not want to get that close to another person. Keeping people at a safe distance works better for me. The word friend is used so loosely. I have tried to become friends with a few others in my life, only to be betrayed. Joseph...well... Joseph was quite young and got himself into a bad situation that night. I just happened to be at the right place at the right time. I just did what I had to do. That is it. I did not expect any reciprocity then, and I do not now."

Vincent interrupted. "An act of heroism."

Jim took a couple of puffs on his cigar and then took another sip.

"Well, I do not think...I would call..,"

Again Vincent interrupted. "Saving his life, from some, some... low life piece of bar...trash. A low life that was drunk and was pissed off because Joseph took a few hundred dollars of his money at the pool table! And he ambushed him in the parking lot with a gun! He would have shot and killed him if it were not for you. Yes, James Patrick, I would call it heroism. You put your life on the line for Joseph. He has never forgotten it. I have never forgotten it. Maria, well...she knows that something happened and that if you had not been in the right place at the right time and were willing to take action, she would have never married the man she was so much in love with and may very well not be at her side as her husband now. She knows that Joseph considers you his friend, and for her, that is all that matters."

They continued to walk for a few minutes of silence, taking a dram every few steps and puffing on their cigars.

Jim, do not get me wrong, she is sharp, or she would not have the position in my company as she does, and she knows that it was not just a minor incident."

More silence as they walked, and Vincent moved his hand across him, telling Jim about his garden. Then he stated to Jim.

"I do not give anything to anyone. They earn it the hard way. That's right, even my daughter! She most likely knows that there is more to the story, but she has never asked, nor will she ask. That is the way things are here. That would be up to Joseph to tell her if he ever does."

They talked, consumed the scotch for the next three hours, and smoked a couple of cigars. Jim answered all of Vincent's questions, expounding on several, giving Vincent an idea of his life as a teacher with no political connections in a very corrupt county in the south and the type of people he had been dealing with. Jim did not hide anything, nor did he lie about anything. He told Vincent of the loss of his daughter, his youngest son, and the devastating loss of his beloved "Twin-Flame." Jim was surprised that Vincent did not ask what he meant by "Twin-Flame." Vincent listened and watched Jim as he related his life in brief.

Their conversation went to insignificant topics for several minutes, and then it returned to a more serious subject: the United States Government. They talked about the social hypocrisy and the religious hypocrisy in the country. Vince learned that James Patrick had a significant problem with religious hypocrisy but did not have any problem with the working women on the street.

On the topic of Washington politics, Jim expressed his utter loathing. Legal corruption, he would tell Vincent. The only organization that can make their own rules, give themselves a raise, make millions from insider information, and cannot be legally touched by anyone! Why? Because the gang of elected officials makes the fucking law! Jim went from politics to religion, setting off a lengthy oratory disdain for any cult aspect. He paused and looked directly at Vincent, "Cults, religious organizations, and political parties are just that. Look the word up. No offense meant."

Then a long period of silence as they walked the grounds again and returned to the gazebo for a refill.

James Patrick was on a roll and had felt at ease and figured he would get his personal feelings thrown into the mix if he wanted to know about him. So Vincent Spadalini listened and, on occasion, would break a slight smile.

Then after several minutes of venting, Jim paused and looked directly at Vincent, took a deep breath, reached for his scotch glass, took a sip, then placed it gently down.

"Sorry, Vincent, just a few touchy subjects and likely too much alcohol, which appears to be loosening up my tongue a bit. Which I normally do not do. But I feel like I am in good company and safe here. I have expounded on subject matters more than my norm."

"Capisco. But it is okay. You are in good company, and you are safe here. And I can appreciate your candidness."

The conversation finally got to the hit on Finkel and how Jim felt about it.

"I have reached the point when it comes to these people, my feelings are the same as when I served in Viet Nam. I feel nothing. It is just business. You are assigned a job to do, and you do it with pride and the greatest expertise possible."

They spoke at length about the relationship between him and Joseph. Where Jim expected to go from the point they were at and at what cost. Vincent Spadalini seemed pleased at Jim's responses to his questions.

They spoke about his retirement, his family, what was left of it, and his feelings toward family. Their conversation turned to his Irish background and the close relationship between the Irish and the Italian culture. They briefly touched on religion, God, and Catholicism. Vincent learned that Jim had no religion and loathed all faiths.

Through the in and out of morals and religion, Vincent learned that he was profoundly spiritual and was told face to face that he would not go into any details about his spiritual ideology.

Vincent could tell that Jim was still troubled by the bad memoirs of long ago. He could tell in his voice that he was bitter about the loss of his family members. Vincent

Spadalini knew that power brokers could make or break people in the game of politics. He also knew that lying and "underhanded" tactics were only part of their weaponry. He also knew that in most cases, most people in a public position, if they were not part of some political party with connections, they were as good as dead, a living death, which was worse than death itself if you placed any value on your family name.

Vincent took over the conversation and turned the conversation to the banking business, shipping, and hotel business as Jim absorbed every word Vincent Spadalini spoke. He would, from time to time, with hesitation, ask a question concerning the companies they were talking about and would get a synopsis of his query.

Then, as some silence occurred, Jim finished his drink, reached into the ice bucket, obtained two ice cubes, dropped them into his glass, and poured himself another dram of whiskey. Vincent watched him, and then he spoke.

James P., I know about the attempt to assassinate you and your wife. And I know why. That got Jim's attention quickly, even though his mind was not working at a hundred percent capacity. With both hands loosely wrapped around his glass as it set on the table, turning it in the same spot slowly, looking down into the fresh glass of scotch, his head tilted, turning it slightly to his left, looking at "Don" Vincent Spadalini out of his left eye. Even in the dim light provided by the elaborate lighting system, set on a medium setting for illumination, which could be adjusted to whatever level one wanted, he could see no bullshit about him in the man's eyes.

"Jim, I know a lot about you, which is why you are here. Joseph and I have had several talks concerning you. Joseph has requested that I meet you personally. I know how you feel about your name. I, too, have very strong feelings about a family name! I think..." Then Vincent finished his drink, refilled his glass with two ice cubes, and poured himself a double scotch.

"I think there is no limit a man should have in defending his family honor, his name. However, I have noticed over the years that fewer people are proud of their family names. Over the years, there has been a saying: what's in a name? Well, there is a lot in a name."

In all that was discussed, never once was Jim questioned about his exact residence or where his son was.

In a part of the conversation, Vincent brought up Brian O'Francis, and Jim learned they were together in the shipping and hotel business. However, he did not elaborate on how they met and the extent of their business. Jim did learn that he and Brian were born in the same part of the country and that their father had the same name. However, Jim also knew that was not uncommon.

Vincent asked Jim if he had any objections to meeting Brian. With a slight bit of hesitation, he replied that he had none. Then, Vince asked Jim if he would object to returning to Chicago in a month or so as he had a business appointment with Brian and would be in the area during that period. James Patrick thought for a few moments as they finished off their scotch.

"I will take care of your expenses. Don't worry about that. I just have a feeling about the two of you. I cannot get over the similarities. I think you will be very surprised. But, bear in mind, there may be nothing to it. However, I still would like you to meet Brian. That is if you have no objections."

"No, sir, I do not. But I do not think…" Then Jim stopped himself. Jim had reservations about the whole conversation but went with his little voice (*stop talking*), which was much clearer than his current mental balance, and agreed to return to meet Brian O'Francis.

As they parted for the night and gave Sophia and their staff a gracious thanks, James P. was still shocked about meeting Vincent Spadalini. He could not get over why he was given such special treatment. He was worldly enough to know that not just every "swinging dick" dined with the head of a "Family" nor had a candid, lengthy conversation with him. To top the entire evening off, to be asked to return to meet someone who just happened to have the same last name that "Don" Vincent Spadalini felt looked like Jim was not natural, not for the world Vincent operated.

Jim spent the next day with Joseph taking a guided tour of the city and the Spadalini empire headquarters.

Michael and Joseph took Jim to the airport on the third morning of his trip. James P. had gotten little sleep his last night in the "Windy City," reviewing all that had been discussed— what he had said, and what Vincent had said. The three said their farewells. "*Til next time*," as Joseph put it.

The Review

James Patrick O'Francis' flight took off on time. Destination: Atlanta, Georgia.

He pondered on the short flight.

Why me? Why would a man like that take the time out of his life for someone like me? What am I not seeing? Who is this Brian O'Francis? Shit...brother...I just do not think so. For us to have the same father? Someone I had never met! The odds of some such event happening in my life, well, hell, ain't no way!

The airline host interrupted his thoughts. Jim took an orange juice, thanked her, and then looked out the window at the passing clouds below him, returning to his thoughts.

This man, hell, Joseph for that matter, well, even Maria, all are way out of my league. I have nothing to offer, not that much money, and I really do not give a damn about the evil bastards that destroyed my career as a teacher and a coach. Tarnishing my family name throughout the entire area is not that important in the real world. What's in a name anymore? Shit, no one really cares! As to what I think, wellll...Hell, I damn sure ain't the one to vindicate the wrong that has been done. I do not understand. Is this my Fate? Naaaa...I do not think...well, why all the right connections now? Are these the right connections? Is this a test? I never really do know. Will I ever? I do not think...I will understand my own philosophy— whatever I have.

However, nothing happens out of coincidence. So there has got to be a reason?

James P. had developed a headache from all the drinking, lack of sleep, and thinking.

He became mentally stressed with his own thoughts, forced his thoughts onto his beloved Dawn, and drifted off to sleep for a short nap.

Upon arriving in Atlanta, he made his way to the Café Intermezzo Cheers restaurant, where he found "The Man" waiting for him. It was 9:15 A.M.

"So, how was your trip?" Paul asked.

"Very interesting. Very interesting, to say the very least."

"How is Vincent Spadalini?"

"Fine, I guess? Hell, I really do not know how to answer that. I mean...I cannot get over me even being there."

"Well, Jim, ole friend, let me tell you something."
Then Paul took a sip of coffee. The waitress arrived and
asked if he would like more coffee and asked Jim if he would
like something to drink and a menu. So he ordered coffee,
and she handed him a menu.

"I'll return in a few minutes."

"Let me tell you about Vincenzo Spadalini. First off,
he knows a lot about you. Second, he liked what he had
learned about you. Third, he can't quite figure you, Jim."

"Figure me? Why? I am nothing. An ex-school teacher
run out of the profession at that! And by the way, how well
do you know him?"

"First, I know him very well. The how, welll, is…?"

Jim interrupted. "That is fine. Shit, I do not want to
know the how. It is not important."

"Now,"… the server arrived, and Jim ordered
breakfast. Three eggs, four pieces of bacon, two slices of
toast, and two pancakes.

As soon as the server walked away, Paul smiled.
"Hungry, are you?"

Jim smiled and had a little chuckle in his voice. Then
he spoke in his best Irish accent. "Well, the point of fact is, I
am. Hell, with all that has happened to me in the last 48
hours, I am stressed, and when I get that way, I eat. 'Tis all

the alcohol I consumed for the past two nights. It makes an Irishman hungry." Then he laughed.

"James P., what puzzled Vincent Spadalini is you never ask for anything."

"Sooooo."

"Well, that is not normal, especially if someone has a lot of money. And shall I say, in the position he is."

"Well, we touched on that matter. I still, at this point, do not see the point in wanting to meet me, and why all the interest in me? I mean, shit, Paul...come on, man, I am out of everyone's picture, doing nothing in a place where no one knows me or anything about me, and I like it like that."

The server brought his food and refilled both coffee cups. Jim thanked her, and she was off.

"I think I can give you some answers. I don't know if I can answer all the questions. However, Joseph took it upon himself to take care of some business without Vincenzo's okay. Now that, one does not do! I don't give a fuck if you are his number one "son." Son-in-law, he is well-entrenched in the hotel and the shipping business, and several other businesses of the Spadalini empire dealings, and I might add does his job extremely well, as does his wife. However, Joseph just wanted to do something for you. I'll not get into why he wanted to, and you know that."

"Yes, yes, I...well, I wish he would have picked Bales...but, at any rate..."

"Well, he knows that was just the tip of the 'iceberg.' Over so many years, the main players in your past problems were untouched, and he has been briefed on them. I am sure he spoke to you as to their future?"

"Yes, but not all the details, just a few comments. There is more to a job than just a few words or wants."

Paul quickly responded. "I know. That is why he wanted to talk to you firsthand. He was assured that you could be trusted and that your words were bonded. I told you he liked what he had learned about you. The man is sharp. Do not let his age fool you; it has many people. Not that his age is old, I mean you and I, you know what I mean. He did not become what he is by making mistakes. Did you like him?" Paul concluded.

"Yes, I did. He and Sophia were extremely gracious, with no facade. That I also question. I am nothing to these people."

"James P.," Paul stated, "these people, as you refer to them, are like everybody. Yes, they are wealthy. Yes, they are in big business, big politics, and high in the social order. However, they can be and are 'down to earth,' if you get my drift? I know from personal experience that they have not forgotten from wince Vincent or Sophia came. In addition, their daughter, well, looks, yes. Class, yes. Rich, yes. Very intelligent, yes, and she has it all. But, no, most are not like her either. Joseph, well, you know him. He did not change after he entered into the 'family.'

"Capisco. To a point. As to Joseph, well, I knew him when. When we were young." Jim stated.

"He is the same Joseph, just the rough edges of the stone have been removed to fit the builder. The builder was Vincent. He is now more honed in the manner that Vincent Spadalini wants. Yet, he still knows where he was raised and why he has what he does. Maria loves him deeply, even with all she has going for her and her age. Shit, she knows she could have had anyone she wanted, and even to this day, she can have anyone she wants. She knew that way back when.

Nevertheless, she had her sights set on Joseph, and by god, she got him. He has come a long way in the business." Paul paused and thought. O'Francis sat, sipped his coffee, consumed his breakfast, and listened.

"Jim, look. The 'Family,' well, it ain't like everything you see on T.V., and all these anti-mob, justice files, bull shit! Good god almighty, I could tell you some stories about our fucking government that would make the 'mob' look like a Boy Scout troop! You damn sure do not see any programs or

[70]

documents about our government and all of its operations. Illegal at that, may I state! Vincenzo's business is...well...for the most part, on the up and up. Moreover, the business of taking care of business, so to speak, well, that too has changed. Now I damn sure ain't going to sit here and blow smoke up your ass. Yes, they do 'take care of business,' but so does our own government, despite all the news media propaganda! It is different than it was, ohhh, thirty or even twenty years ago."

James P. finished his meal, accepted another cup of coffee, and requested his bill.

"Fine, I think. I am not sure, but I think I get the idea." Jim responded to end the conversation.

Paul asked if he had all his tickets for his return flight to his now semi-private world.

"Hey, don't worry; you'll be safe where you are. I know these things. You're safe!"

"One more thing before we go, did Vincent speak of Brian?"

Jim's eyes quickly locked on Paul's, and the look on his face told everything. "Yes!"

They rose and walked out into the open area of the corridor. It was somewhat of a walk to the boarding area. As Jim commented on the rather large mobile hanging from the top of the building, always seeing the art in almost everything. Some small talk again took place, assurance of his safety and privacy.

"James P.," Paul stated, "Vincent Spadalini is very big on a man's word and a code of honor, another point he liked about you." The two shook hands, and as they did, Paul's thumb slipped to a spot on Jim's right hand. Paul smiled. Jim did not. He just looked at Paul.

"Yes, James P., I am. Take me as I take you."

Jim still did not speak. Nor did he move his thumb. Then, finally, they broke their hands, and Paul said as he placed his hand on Jim's left shoulder.

"I'll be in touch. Enjoy your trip home. I will explain in full in due time. Just wait, a time of patience, and all will be revealed. Capisci?"

O'Francis had broken just the slightest of a smile. He did not speak. He turned and walked away.

Damon's Attack on Patrick

Last summer, Damon Bales was at Honsburg High. Patrick O'Francis entered his first year of high school. He had not had a very good eighth-grade year, and his self-esteem was at rock bottom. His grades had slipped, and his desire for education was in the darkest hole one could imagine. But unfortunately, it only takes one or two teachers to derail any student and send them spiraling down the dark tunnel of ignorance.

For Patrick, this had happened once in elementary school with a "dead-wood" worthless person that the system called a "teacher," which was so bad that it made dead-wood seem solid and vibrant.

Then it occurred again in his junior high year with a teacher that did more damage to students than anyone in education could imagine—just another example of the quality of education in Reynolds County.

Damon made a point of looking up the records of Jim and Dawn's son Patrick. He removed his file, took it to the guidance department, and ordered them to place him in the School Drop Out and At-Risk Program.

The guidance counselor called the O'Francis home.

"Coach, this is Howard. How are you doing?"

Knowing that Howard did not call him to wish him a good day or see if his health was good, he knew something was wrong the second Howard started talking. He informed James Patrick that he or Dawn needed to come to the school and meet with the SDARP director and was informed why.

Dawn's work hours were from 11:00 A.M. to 11:00 P.M., so Jim had to tell her what he had learned at work.

After a few phone calls and some legal checking, they learned that the parents had to consent in writing before a child could be placed in such a program. In addition, they discovered that reasons for establishing a student in such a program had to be documented by several teachers.

Jim did a quick and very intense investigation into the program itself. He learned that the students in such a program were from broken homes, alcohol/drug abusive parents, students with a history of violence in the house, parents who sexually abused them, and students with a history of violence in the classroom.

Dawn walked into Howard's office. "Good morning Howard," she stated with a big smile. "I understand Patrick is being placed in a special class." Her voice was warm and friendly.

"Mrs. O'Francis, now, this was not my idea. I want you to know that."

"Well, you are the guidance counselor, and I understand that this new program for at-risk students must go through you. So, if you had nothing to do with Patrick getting put into such a program, who placed him there?"

Howard became nervous and started stuttering, never giving her an answer but directing Dawn to the program's head for her scheduled appointment.

As she entered the room with Howard leading the way, a large smile came across Dawn's face. Leigh Peng, the daughter of "Shihan" William Peng, was sitting behind the desk. After Howard introduced Dawn, Leigh played the role and went along with the scene without prompting. Howard escaped as quickly as if he was a gust of wind that had blown through the open window.

Before Dawn sat down, Leigh asked, "I have to ask Dawn," holding the file of Patrick O'Francis up in the air. "What in the hell is this?"

"Leigh, I don't have a clue."

"Well, I knew it had to be some dumb-ass that placed Patrick's name on the list. I mean, of all people, a father like he's got. Hell, Dawn, that is an insult to my father! But, of course, these people don't know I know you and Jim.

Moreover, they most likely do not know who my father is. Nor that Jim is and has been one of his students for years. Christ! What a fucking joke!" Then she began to laugh, as did Dawn.

"So, Leigh, who did put him on the list?"

"Well, the only people that saw this list are the counselor, principal, and secretary. So you can figure. Not too hard, huh?"

"No, not at all," Dawn replied, smiling.

"Why? I know everyone knows how he feels about James P. Well, unless you are dead from the neck up.

However, to attack your son, I mean, is evil! And Dawn, that is just what this is, an attack on your son!"

"Well, Leigh, this school has been dealing with evil for the past six years! And yes, he is mean! He is evil, mean!" Dawn's tone of voice had changed to a more serious one.

"Wellll, I think I have found that this student is not the kind we are looking for. So he does not qualify for this program."

Then she laughed again. Dawn momentarily placed her right-hand palm outward over her forehead and in a sad voice.

"Oooooh, Leigh, I am so broken up over this. I really..." and she could not go any further as Dawn began to laugh along with Leigh.

A Siblings Request

The phone rang, and Patrick answered. Most children beat their parents to the phone, basically because they make little effort to challenge for the privilege of being the ones to say hello or some off-the-wall line like, "your quarter," used to be a dime, "you called, you talk." Or some of the older, "moldy" sayings like, "morgue, you stab'em, we slab'em," "Jake's pool hall, eight ball speaking," "hello, grape-vine, what's the juice." On the other end was Dawn's sister, Theresa, and then you would hear, "Mom, its Theresa," and for the next hour and often as long as two hours, depending on how much "catching up" the two had to do, Dawn was on the phone. On this day, the call was more serious and would require a great deal of talk between Jim and Dawn.

Theresa and Dennis had a great deal of trouble with their youngest son Nicodemus who was the same age as Patrick, soon to be fourteen, and needed help. City life was taking its toll on Nicodemus. Poor grades in school, problems related to teachers and other students, suspensions, and gang-related connections on the street drove both parents to make a substantial request to Jim and Dawn.

Would they take Nicodemus in and get him through school? They felt that the change in environment would change his lifestyle and attitude. But, before asking, they knew that Nico and Jim would cross sabers because of the strict rules in the O'Francis home. They knew that was asking a great deal of Dawn and Jim, but they were at the end of their rope.

They hoped they could save their son from the violence and crime that seemed to be attracting him like a moth to a flame, only to be burned and his life destroyed. But unfortunately, it would not be an easy task, as Dawn's mother had moved into the house with them only two years earlier, and that in itself was taking a toll on Jim and Dawn, even though it was her mother. "Maw-maw," as Jim referred to her, was not the easiest person to live with. Gloria was set in her ways and very reluctant to change or adapt. In addition, Gloria was reared in an old Italian family, making for some difficult times in the O'Francis home.

Plus, she had suffered through WWII and migrated from the totalitarian grip of Mussolini to England. She was then living through the bombing of London by the dictatorial regime of Hitler. So between Jim's mother-in-law's PTSD and his, there were some tense moments in the O'Francis home.

He related the story to me and how Nicodemus made it into his home. I asked him why he would take on such an enormous task and was already under pressure and stress. His response did not surprise me, given that I had learned a great deal about the man by that point. As he would often do, he took a deep breath and leaned over on the top rail of the deck, looking out over the short field leading into the forest, usually taking a puff or two off his cigar.

"Well, I did give it a lot of thought, and Dawn and I hashed it over before I gave my okay. But it had to be under my terms, and I had already helped so many teens that were not even related to me, adopted, or married into the family, I guess is a better way of putting it. So, I decided that I could save one more teen heading for a jail cell or death, whichever came first."

Cousins Kuntz

The two families met in Dayton, Ohio, at their cousin's home, Dennis and Theresa at Barbie's, and Jim and Dawn at Jean's house.

After a long evening of talk, drinks, and food, and still mixed into the seriousness of the matter, a lot of fun and laughter, jokes, and the Kuntz craziness, which Jim had habituated himself to over the years. The final test would come the next day with a meeting with the young "stud" and Uncle O'Francis.

James P. and Nicodemus went for a long walk along the levee of the Miamisburg River. He laid out the rules to the young street-smart boy or thought he was the tough street hood. James P. did not mix any words. He addressed him on an equal basis, and Nico found that the old (in his mind) man had some of the "street" in him. He was stunned to learn that Uncle O'Francis was not so "dumb" about "what is happening" as he had once thought. He agreed that he would abide by the rules of the O'Francis house and that any deviation would result in some degree of punishment.

While Jim was off on his walk and talked to Nicodemus, Dawn told her sister that it would all be up to how Nicodemus responded to their talk. Even though the sisters were extremely close, it was not her call.

Theresa's greatest fear was that they would return from their walk, and James P. would say, "No." But, of course, he would have if he had not felt that he could save the boy, and she and Dennis both knew him well enough that he could and would say "no" if he did not feel that there was at least a chance for Nicodemus.

So the city boy was headed for the country. The Stepanian family was very grateful.

Jim had given much thought to the new principal at Honsburg high school, Henry Stafford. He had gotten along very well with him at one time as a teaching colleague, but things seemed to have changed.

Henry was not as stupid as people thought he was. After going through several women in the school system, he had zeroed in on Rose Bassel, a P.E. teacher with the personality of a sour dishrag. Her social upbringing in one of the three wealthiest families in Honsburg gave her an attitude of superiority over the rest of the community and the school. She rarely spoke to O'Francis the entire time he had been at the high school. Her years at the elementary school had not been pleasant for her colleagues, who were happy to see her transferred to the high school.

Henry started his move on her in O'Francis' last two years of coaching. It took him about a snap of a finger to figure out Henry's move. The political connections and her money all equal power.

Henry had started to "turn" to the LaMar Marshy side of the game shortly after his marriage to Rose. Jim did not trust Henry, but if he wanted to teach on a high school level again and coach, he would have to play the Reynolds County political game. *Adapt and overcome*, he would tell himself.

Therefore, off he went to pay an unannounced visit to Henry to discuss the new arrival into the O'Francis home, giving Henry a brief on Nicodemus and requesting that he help in any professional way. Letting Jim know if there were any problems, even the smallest ones, they might head off some major disaster.

Henry seemed very receptive to O'Francis and assured him that he would help in any way.

As O'Francis ended the conversation, he congratulated Henry on his promotion to principal. Jim also asked Henry if he had any problems with him requesting to return to the coaching ranks and return to the high school level. Henry assured him that he had no issues with either request. And would accept him if the request was approved. However, he went one step further than Jim had expected.

Just as O'Francis was at the door, Henry stated;

"Jim, one more thing. I want you to know that I think you were a damn good teacher and a damn good coach. I have seen you in both positions firsthand, and I would attest to this fact. The problems with you and Damon do not reflect how I feel. I want you to know that."

Jim smiled, nodded his head up and down, and left. Knowing that he, too, would do precisely as Führer Marshy instructed.

The following week, Jim learned that Henry had fired Richard Finkel from his coaching and Athletic Director's positions. Notifying him that he needed to start looking for another teaching position. He did not want him at school at the beginning of the following year.

Hourglass

The phone rang…"Hello."

"Bruce, Brian here."

"Haaa… how ya been lately."

"Bruce, I need a job done. Do you have some time?"

"Yes."

Bruce ran all security for all of Brian's hotels throughout the county and several other large firms and businesses.

"My jet will be there, uhh, let's say…tomorrow at 1500 hours. Can you make that?" There was a short pause.

"Yes, no problem. What's the equipment?"

"A camera, and of course, your choice of weaponry. All other information will be handed to you when you get there."

Bruce knew all accommodations, a file, transportation, and a driver would be handled. This was not anything new for him, and he worked side jobs for Brian many times over the many years he had known him and was at his disposal at a moment's notice. Bruce also knew that a lot of "recon" work would go into any mission he had. He expected no mistakes. Bruce had made none over the years, and all assignments were successful. Bruce also knew his people would be called on later to finish the job. Rarely did he do any "heavy work" anymore. He had four professionals who were masters at their professional skills doing "physical labor." His job was to gather all information, plan the operation, and make the assignments.

The private jet taxied to a stop outside a hangar. A few minutes later, the door opened and a well-dressed gentleman emerged in beige dress slacks, a black turtleneck, a brown tweed jacket, and tan and brown Italian-made loafers. The six-foot-two, two-hundred-thirty-pound man, stood at the bottom of the steps. His gray-white hair, with some black still intertwined and receding hairlines on both sides that he now brushed straight back, touched the top of his jacket on his neck. He had dark eyebrows and a full dark mustache tapering down each side of his lips with a tent of gray at the ends. He stood very erect, and his dark skin displayed his entire head. His face was stern and expressionless as he watched the approaching car. It stopped three feet from him, and the passenger window came down, "Welcome to the mountains, Mr. Beck."

He leaned down slightly, peered into the car, and then a smile broke across his face. The trunk popped open, and he put his two pieces of luggage and a camera bag in it and closed the lid. Within minutes they were on the interstate headed north.

Arrangements were made for him to stay at the Courtyard Marriott Suites. Paul had secured a room in his name and took Bruce to it, and then they walked fifty yards to O'Charley's restaurant for dinner. After a few hours of bar time and several drinks, the schedule was set.

It was 0600 hours when they left the hotel. Their first stop on tour was the area of Carl Decal's house. With a Canon camera and an assortment of lenses, including a 500 mm lens, he could take as many pictures covertly as he needed of the area, roads, intersections, businesses, and individuals. He took several of the Decal home on all sides, the surrounding terrain, and the street entering the lavish subdivision.

At 0800 hours, Carl came out his front door and walked to get his paper, and the camera clicked off pictures.

At 1000 hours, the garage door opened, and Carl backed his silver BMW out of his garage and drove off. Bruce clicked off several shots of his license plate, giving some space between them, and in ten minutes, they arrived at Lowe's. As Carl walked toward the entrance, Bruce took several more pictures.

The following day, it was mid-afternoon before Carl, and his wife emerged from their seven hundred-thousand-dollar home. The couple headed north on the rural two-lane highway in their tan four-door Mercedes-Benz and traveled for a good hour and a half deep into the lush green mountains of the southern Appalachian Mountain Range.

Bruce spoke of the beauty of the mountains and asked about the strips of land carved out of the tops of the mountains. Even though Bruce knew what strip mining was, he had never been in an area where it had taken place. Paul explained that it was known as strip mining. He then elaborated on how and why it had been a significant money-making source for an elite group of people who were very rich from the 1970s through the 1980s.

Bruce opened a file. "I read this report on Mr. Decal last night." He turned several pages and then ran his finger down the page, "Here, it says he got out of education, uhh, in 1987, correct?"

As Paul drove, he paused in thought. "I believe that is correct."

"Well, why did this man continue to involve himself with James P. O'Francis and his efforts to better himself? I see nothing on O'Francis giving him cause...or is there something I should know?"

"No. O'Francis is clear on that part."

"Well, Paul, it really did not make a damn to me. I don't know any of these people. I'm here to assess and ensure the job will be done correctly. I don't give a damn who did what to whom! Not my call, you know that."

"Well, Bruce, I know, and as to the why on Decal, I really don't know. Jim was never a threat to him and his little power structure. He wanted to be part of O'Francis's fall and disgrace his name. But, I do know that he did not like him."

"Why?"

"Basically, because he could not control O'Francis, Jim would not kiss his ass and place him on a high god-like pedestal as everyone else did. Some ego trip he was on. He was one of those people who worked in the backdrop, using others, the weak and stupid, to do his dirty work."

"I can see by this report that it cost O'Francis a rather high price, not in dollars per say, by our standards. And by the way, are these figures correct?"

"Which figures are you talking about?"

"The ones on this man's salary?"

"You mean O'Francis's salary?"

"Yes, on page ten of your report, you stated what he made and lost as a family."

"Yes, the figures are on the mark." Bruce looked out the window, a rather long pause in their conversation, then back at the figures on the pages in front of him, and then back out the window. Paul drove the mountain road, then looked over at him.

"Something bothering you, Bruce?"

He slowly closed the file. "Well, yes, as a matter of fact, it is." A thirty-second pause. "I had forgotten what it was like not to have money. This guy, O'Francis, I mean, shit...this man don't or didn't have a pot to piss in! Is he, or was he a teacher? I mean, I thought..."

Paul interrupted, "You thought teachers made more money than that, correct?"

"Correct."

"You have been out of touch with the lower-middle-income people of the world Bruce. Look, I really did not know either. I was working on a case and came in contact with O'Francis accidentally! Our world, and his...Christ, man...well, they are a planet apart, believe me. You just are not used to the common people, nor was I. We have been involved in the upper political and business world of high finance, and it really is an eye-opener to step down to the world Jim once existed in."

Then there was another short pause as Bruce looked at the mountain scenery.

"As to what he has lost, well...yes, in some people's eyes, it may not mean much, but to James P., it meant a lot. See...well, you must understand something here...Jim lived by a code that really doesn't fit in this day and time. Hell, for that matter, it did not fit in the '70s, '80s, or '90s. O'Francis is a rare breed of a man, and that is why, as trivial as it may seem, you are here. He is not, nor has he ever been, an important person, politically or business-wise. But, for some reason..." Then Paul paused as Bruce Beck changed lenses and snapped more pictures of some of the landscape.

Paul continued, "He touches people and has affected their lives in the simplest ways. He never asked for anything in return other than letting him do his job. Jim's problem was he was too honest and too damn candid. He could not play the political game in Reynolds County, where some malicious people hurt innocent people. He and his family are one."

"Okay, how is it that one teacher makes so little, and you have this Decal person living in a half-million-dollar plus home in a multi-million dollar sub-division?"

"Don't get the two confused, Bruce. Decal got his money from his wife. Her father left it to her. Her father was in the mining business and made a lot of money. So Carl Decal really did not have to teach. He could have lived off his wife's money."

"Then why did he choose to give O'Francis a hard time?"

"Well, the best I can figure is he did not like him, as I have stated. He felt he was a threat to his over-inflated ego. Basically, Decal is a real ass-hole! For several years, I have followed his work and efforts to character-assassinate O'Francis. He did a real job on him."

Bruce looked over at Paul, took a drink of water, and said, "And people believed this Decal?"

Paul then stated, "He is smooth. He is about as spineless as they come. His mouth is more dangerous than a cocked pistol."

Bruce had placed the file between his seat and the center console.

"Not that it matters, Paul, but is O'Francis some little college book worm?"

Paul laughed. "No. No, by no means! I realize you're just here to do a job, and you are just curious, but he is nothing like that."

Paul then briefed him on a few points of James P. and his military background, his obsession with the martial arts, and his love for teaching and helping teens. His effort was to change his life and put his past behind him. Paul included a few items of his coaching as part of his teaching.

Bruce listened intently, and when Paul finished, he just grunted and said, "Hmmmmm, I see. Sounds like a man who could have been one of us? Any connection to Brian?"

Bruce changed lenses again and snapped off several pictures, bringing his camera to his eye and focusing on the home the Decals had arrived at.

"Very interesting, this O'Francis is. Very interesting."

The two men then drove back to the city. Paul addressed some of the people on the list and how many times Bruce would be requested to return to the area before all the pieces were in place.

They arrived back at the hotel, and as Bruce was getting out of the car, bending down at the waist with his right hand on the top of the opened door and looking back into the car, asking, "I'll see you for dinner, correct?"

"Yes, let's make it around eight. I have some work I need to do."

"Okay, ahh, Paul..." Bruce asked again, "Jim and Brian related?"

Paul paused as he looked out the front window and then back at Bruce. "I don't know, Bruce." Bruce never moved, as there was a ten-second pause in their conversation.

"Bruce, I think you and Brian should talk about it. I mean, it is not my place to discuss that."

Bruce affirmatively nodded his head, closed the door, and walked to the hotel entrance.

The Legal Game

Holly set up the time for the deposition for both Damon Bales and Richard Finkel. James P. arrived at the attorney's office thirty minutes before the deposition. Holly pulled him aside.

"Now, Jim, I want you to sit and say nothing. You can't. If you want me to ask something, write it down and pass it to me. Look, they will say things that will get you upset. Do not show your emotions. Let me deal with them. We will review all they say later, okay?"

Jim had never been in a deposition, and he was not ready for what he would hear, but he would do what Holly requested. So he instantaneously put his mind on a major self-control mode, preparing himself for the worst, and it came.

In the next four hours, he would hear more lies and more denials than he had ever heard in any one period of time, all under oath. The one thing that struck him about the court system was the words 'swear to God.' So much for the legal system and the swearing thing.

O'Francis felt it was the height of hypocrisy.

O'Francis laughed several times when Holly redirected her questions earlier in the deposition and got different answers. He found it very odd that Richard stated he was not afraid, nor was he intimidated by his conversation with O'Francis on the morning in question. Jim thought to himself as Holly went on.

"Well, dumb-ass, if that is the case, then why did you take the events that occurred to Bales?"

Holly returned to the fact that it had not bothered Richard Finkel and asked, "Mr. Finkel, if this confrontation with Mr. O'Francis did not intimidate you as you stated, and you were not in fear of your health or your life, then why did you take the event that took place on the date in question to Mr. Bales?"

Richard twisted and turned in his seat, not like before when he had puffed up his chest like a giant toad and played the macho man for Holly.

"I really don't know. I guess, well, I thought Mr. Bales should know."

"Well, Mr. Finkel, if it was that important, why did you wait five days before you brought this to the attention of Mr. Bales?"

"Well, I did not have time."

"According to your statement to Mr. Bales, you feared for your well-being. And you are telling me that you did not have time."

"Well, Mr. Bales was not at school on the days I was there. Or I was absent when he was there."

"I see. Tell me, Mr. Finkel, do you have a phone?"

"Well, yes, I do."

"Okay, does Mr. Bales have a phone?"

"I suppose he does."

"You suppose he does."

"Well, yes, I have never been in his house."

"Have you ever had an occasion to call Mr. Bales at his home after school hours?"

There was a long pause before Richard answered.

"Mr. Finkel," Holly sternly stated, "you might want to think about how you will answer that question very carefully."

"Well, yes, I have called him at home."

"If the events at the service station were so life-threatening to you, and you and Mr. Bales could not see each other at school, then why didn't you pick up the phone and call him?"

"Uhh, I don't know. Don't guess I thought of it."

Damon, of course, had a loss of memory on many questions. Although, when it came to typing the letter, he could remember that and proudly stated to Holly how many words a minute he could type and how many he could type when he was in high school.

All that did not impress Holly. Damon admitted sending the letter to the School Board, Superintendent, and all the various law enforcement agencies in the area.

When asked why he sent the letters, he responded, "Ms. Donatello," always drawing out the Ms. part when he addressed her. "Terrorist acts have been conducted against me. He has threatened Mr. Finkel. We feared for our lives and that of other teachers in the school. They feared for their lives."

"Do you know that any or all of these so-called terrorist acts involved Mr. O'Francis?"

"Welll, now, I feel that they do."

"But Mr. Bales, I asked you if you had any facts to back up your statement that terrorist acts allegedly committed against you and as you say others, including Mr. Finkel, were committed by Mr. O'Francis."

"Mssss. Donatello, I believe they could have very easily been!"

"Then, if you were in such fear for your lives, why did you and Mr. Finkel wait so long to create this letter, now in front of you, and send it out to the various legal organizations you have done?"

Bales danced around the "mulberry tree," never giving a complete and straight answer to her question.

Holly hammered them hard and found lots of flaws in their answers. Bales indicated that many parents had filed many complaints against O'Francis. But when it came to naming all the parents that had filed complaints against O'Francis, he could not recall any names.

Jim felt his attack on his coaching was a major mistake. Bales alleged that officials had called and complained about O'Francis' conduct on the baseball field.

"What were the names of the umpires that called and filed these alleged complaints?"

"Uhh, I do not recall their names at this time."

"Will you recall their names later?"

"I may."

"Well, Mr. Bales, when you recall, I want a copy of all complaints and the names of the parents that filed the complaints."

She looked toward Bales's attorney. He nodded in compliance.

Jim had done enough research to obtain knowledge in the legal game to know that providing any evidence relating to complaints would never occur.

There was a slight pause in Holly's questions as she looked through a few notes she had made. As she leafed through notes, silence permeated the room.

Then out of the mendacious mouth of Damon Bales, "Ms. Donatello, I have had so many parents come to me on numerous occasions and request that Mr. O'Francis be removed as a coach that it is difficult for me to recall them all. Why, several asked if I could have him removed from the school as a teacher."

Holly asked. "What reasons would they give?"

Damon took a deep breath and let it out as if he was tired of all the questions.

"They claimed that he was rude to them, unfair to their sons, and used bad language all the time. That he did not believe in God. His teaching methods were not suited for this area."

Jim sat and took the verbal assault. His abdomen muscles were as tight as the top of a drum. The temples of his head throbbed in pain, and his jaws hurt from the pressure of gritting his teeth. His hands tingled as if needles were piercing them. His desire to exterminate all on the opposite side of the table from him was almost overwhelming.

His phycologist, Dr. Celia Flora, had done for him as much as she could and had helped him with most of his anger issues; as a result, Jim had improved somewhat over a year. But there was nothing she could do for his PTSD. Jim would have to come to terms with it. However, enduring such character assassination tested his ability not to lose control of his inner-most desires even in the presence of his attorney. Holly sensed Jim's impulses, and on several occasions, she discreetly would pat her hand on Jim's left thigh.

During the deposition, Bales stated that the head coaches of baseball and football had requested that Jim O'Francis be removed from their staff. The bold statement left Jim asking himself why. He knew of no actual conflicts between either Harper or Hobart that would warrant dismissal from either one of their staff. Nevertheless, his job performance went beyond the norm. So, if the statement were true, the question for James P. O'Francis was, why?

O'Francis went home and fixed himself several stiff double scotches and tried hard to block out all that he had heard. All the evilness he felt was present in the room.

But, even with a half a fifth gone by bedtime, he got little sleep, and his warrior instinct surfaced in its total capacity, leaving him mentally drained and exhausted by morning.

Into The Fog

Rusty and Jim talked after their briefing giving them their next mission.

"Jim, I fucking hate going into river valleys. I hate it. I hate fucking rivers."

"Well, Rus, in many ways, I also do. But, hell, I grew up on a damn river. I swore to myself that I would never live on one after leaving home."

The mission was not a fun "Tom Sawyer" adventure. In two days, the recon team was to descend on the Da Ja tributary of the Dak Poko River. Walking distance from the Dak Pek camp, approximately 1000 kilometers from the base. "It is not much more than a check," Jim told Rus.

"Yea, yea, I know. Just to make sure they are not getting too close if there is any activity in our immediate area. I get it. But I hate river valleys."

It started raining at high noon on the day before the patrol departed for a short two-day recon up the river toward its headwaters, which put them in the country of Laos.

A heavy fog had set in by the time the six-man patrol was on their way. It was late afternoon with no sun, dim light, and darkness would fall in upon them sooner than usual.

They had a location they wanted to be for observation as it was suspected that there were activities on the river to the north of the camp.

Jim O'Francis (Ranger) took the point, then 20 feet back was Sergeant Robert Burns (SF), and as the line extended was Y-Bon ("Yard"), Rusty Skelton (Ranger), and Y-Jar ("Yard"), and Sergeant Dustin Derek (SF). 'Double D,' as he was referred to.

As the patrol went through the heavy fog, it swirled around them as they punched a hole in the vapors. The fog traveled behind each one for several feet as if the droplets had a life of their own, reaching out to touch each patrol member.

The visibility was no more than ten feet. The patrol uses red lenses on their flashlights to communicate when needed. When Jim felt or heard movement or a sound that was not natural to the river jungle, he used two flashes to stop in place.

It took the "Rain-Maker" patrol to get to their designated co-ordinance longer than expected. Darkness had engulfed the valley. Jim had difficulty following the directions they had on the topo map. He had to stop more often than he wanted. Using their red lens on the flashlights, he and Robert plotted the path needed to get to the location they needed to be: a hollow to the left side of the river. They got settled in for the night one hundred yards up from the bank of the river.

Even "Charlie" would not attempt traveling the river valley because the fog was so heavy. So it was going to be a peaceful night. Wet, chilly, but without activity.

The fog began to lift in the late morning, and then a light drizzle began to fall. The "Rain Maker" patrol started up the river bank at 1000 hours.

Again, Jim was at the point of the patrol. They could see along the banks where activity had been taking place. It was not hard to follow the tracks of the VC up the river. The patrol moved rapidly but cautiously along the banks. After two klicks (one mile), the path and the fresh tracks turned up into the thick jungles of the Annamite Mountain Range.

Jim did not know whether he hated the semi-openness of the river banks or the thick jungles where one could not see from any distance. He had to depend on his acute hearing for any VC patrols coming or going. But, on the other hand, they did not have to be as cautious as the "Rain Maker" patrol. After all, it was their "playground."

By late afternoon, with a dark over-cast, the fog began setting in, limiting visibility. Nevertheless, the "Rain Maker" patrol followed a well-used trail not more than a meter wide (three feet), with the foliage touching them as they ascended the side of the mountain.

It was apparent for the "Rain Maker" patrol that lots of activity occurred. However, there were no wheel tracks, only small arms transported and stored close to Dak Pek.

As Jim reached the top of the ridge, he halted the recon team. They sat and listened for ten minutes. Then O'Francis dropped back to Sergeant Burns, serving his third tour of duty in Viet Nam. O'Francis informed him that the trail forked: one led over the ridge and the other led north along the top of the ridge. They both took the time to plot the tail on their topographic maps. Jim had moved Y-Bon to the trail fork to listen for any approaching VC.

They chose to take the ridgeline for further reconning. A little over a klick and one half, the team found a place to settle for the night: a large outcropping with concaved rock formations just a few meters off the ridge. It gave everyone a dry shelter for at least one night. Unfortunately, the drizzle continued, and the fog covered the valley and the entire mountain area.

Jim saw a brake in the overcast sky as the sun was doing its best to penetrate the mist that blankets the mountains. Then, thanks to the good weather god, a slight breeze swept over the tops of the mountains, shifting the fog elsewhere south of their location. By 1300 hours, the intermitting clouds allowed the sun's heat to penetrate the sparse opening along the top of the ridge.

Far down into the valley on the opposite side of the river, they could see smoke rising into the air, and as the light wind would shift from time to time and send the breeze the team's way, they could smell the smoke. An indication that there was most likely a VC camp far down on the valley floor.

However, all good things must come to an end. After plotting the approximate location of what was believed to be an encampment, the team headed back in the direction they came. Y-Jar took the point, and O'Francis replaced 'Double D' to bring up the rear of the patrol.

As they approached the forks of the trail, Y-Jar came face to face with two VC patrols meeting at the top of the ridge. One was coming up from the river valley, and one from the opposite valley where they had seen and smelled the smoke.

From O'Francis's position, 18 or so meters (60 feet), he heard Y-Jar yell out in his native dialect and open fire.

The six-man recon team scrambled to the left and the right of the trail running atop the ridge and headed toward Y-Jar. O'Francis took the riverside of the mountain. As the bullets struck foliage, the popping and whizzing passed by his left and right and over Jim's head. He quickly got within sight of the VC patrol, took a temporary position behind a tree, and opened fire. He dropped two VCs and fired at random toward the incoming rounds from the VC patrol. As Jim was quickly changing his magazine, a 7.62 round cut through his right fatigues under his armpit, he slapped the magazine into its slot, one round passed through his left pouch pocket on his fatigues.

He moved forward for ten meters. Then, seeing several VC rushing up the trail, having a semi-clear shot, he took the next three out of the "game." Then as quickly as the silence of the mountain jungle had exploded into a violent noise, it became silent once again. Jim never moved. He was lying on his left side on the floor of the jungle mountainside, his right leg outstretched, his right foot dug into the earth, his left leg folded under his right knee. He lay listening, watching for any type of movement. No one was talking.

O'Francis moved another five meters to the edge of the trail leading down the riverside of the mountain. The dead bodies lay scattered on the path in front of him. Jim whistled for Rusty, a whistle the two had established for one another to communicate when necessary. He waited. Jim whistled again. Moments later, he received the answer he was listening for, which meant Rusty was alive. All six members of the "Rain Maker" patrol remained in place for ten more minutes.

Sergeant Barnes was the first to call out to O'Francis. Check-in for all, Jim and Robert found Y-Jar being attended to by Rusty. He had been hit twice, once in his left upper shoulder and one through the right side of his abdomen. By all appearances, it had gone straight through.

"We need to be on the move. These fireworks will bring more VC." Sergeant Burns stated. 'Double D' pulled out the commo from Y-Bon's back. Sergeant Derek connected with the base camp, giving Captain Thompson a SETREP. As Sergeant O'Francis looked at Burns, he noticed his left shoulder down to his elbow was blood-soaked. A round had passed through the muscle of his left outer shoulder.

"Okay," Derek said, "they will send a team to meet us in the valley for added insurance."

As tough as the Montagnard were, Y-Jar needed help getting down to the valley floor and back to base camp.

Celia Flora

Jim's trip to Dr. Celia Flora came at the appropriate time. With his trips back to the land that was once called 'In Country' and the evilness he felt going through a lengthy deposition, he needed some independent-minded person to talk to and receive some unbiased feedback. In their talk, he told his psychologist about the deposition and what he saw and felt. Jim wanted to know if he or it was possible to sense evil.

He never really knew if she was telling him the truth or just patronizing him, but she agreed that some people could detect evil when in their presence and that he could have a special gift.

She warned Jim that it could be a curse to have such a gift and that he had to be very careful about using it.

Dr. Celia Flora sat in her chair in silence for several minutes.

"Jim," she stated slowly, "Evil is out there, and IF you can detect it in other people, you cannot let them know. You will be in danger, as well as your family. Evil is not something to take lightly. It can come in all forms and portrays itself as being pure and very deceiving to the vast majority of the people."

Again, there was a long silence in the room.

Jim slowly started with pauses in between his words.

"I have made several trips back to Viet Nam in the last two weeks. Unfortunately, they were not all pleasant."

Dr. Flora waited for him to continue. He did not.

"So, Jim, what shall we do about these visits?"

"Well, Doc, there is not a damn thing we can do about them. I have no control over what invades my sub-conscience during my slumbering hours. I wish I did. I would damn sure block them from entering my mental room and mess up my day hours of awareness. But unfortunately, it often takes me days to get over these visits. I cannot just erase them like one would a chalkboard."

"Jim, we will begin working on that. Do you want to tell me about your visit?"

"No. I do not believe it will do me any good to be re-visiting what I do not want to visit. I do not think you would understand. For you, or for that matter, to understand, you would have had to be there. Experience the horrors. Words do no good. Telling someone does me or anyone else any good. They are just words and bad memories!"

The Bible Thumper

Jim's students filed into their homeroom fifteen minutes before the school day ended. James Patrick stood in the hallway beside the door. A teacher from the elementary section of the school approached Jim.

"Mr. O'Francis, I would like a moment of your time." Jim did not respond, as her approach and demeanor indicated he did not want to converse with Ms. Raker.

"I have been informed that you do not believe in God and Jesus Christ, our Savior."

James Patrick still did not speak.

"Well, Mr. O'Francis, do you or don't you?"

Jim looked down at the woman, who stood only 5'2" inches. "Ms. Raker, my ideology should not be a concern of yours."

Her voice became sterner. "Well, no atheist should be teaching our children."

Jim started to take the often-used quote by Samuel Clemens (*Never get into an argument with an idiot, they will drag you down to their level and beat you with experience.*) and turn and walk into his classroom, and closed the door in her face. However, knowing how the rumor mill operated within the school and the community, he opted for an educational moment.

"Ms. Raker, to enlighten you as to your lack of knowledge and improve your education about a subject matter that should not be discussed without knowledge of the subject matter. Also, to pass along to your source so they can be enlightened, I do not believe in any organized religion or its cult ideologies. However, I am a spiritual person, and I believe in Druidism. Ms. Raker, you have a lovely rest of the day."

Ms. Raker stood with her mouth open, looking up at Jim O'Francis. Jim turned and walked into his classroom, closing the door in her face.

Blood Line

Brian O'Francis arrived at Chicago's O'Hare airport a day before his scheduled meeting with Vincenzo Spadalini. His chauffeur was waiting for him at the hangar where his private plane was stored and took his bags.

Exiting the airport area, he took his boss via interstate W 90 to 31 to 14 North to Crystal Lake, where he had a home off North Shore Drive overlooking the lake.

Brian O'Francis stood six foot one inch tall and weighed one hundred and ninety-plus pounds. Salt and pepper hair, more graying on the sides than anywhere, some receding in his hairline. He kept his hair short and parted it in the middle. He had a medium complexion and a solid framed body, clean-shaven except for a black mustache that extended to each corner of his mouth, just starting to get some gray appearing in it.

Brian was all business and a very successful businessman. He started his career in the hotel business and had very lucrative ties in several hotel chains, aside from the outright ownership of several of his own. In addition, he had gotten interested in the shipping business, Great Lakes

Shipping, or "Lakers," as the Great Lake's people knew them in that business. Which by "fate" had led to Vincent Spadalini, and a partnership was born.

Brian K. O'Francis's service days were with the Navy SEALs. The SEALs' ancestry dates back to WWII, known as Navy "Fog men." The SEALs were born from John Kennedy's belief that unconventional warfare was needed to aid and assist the more conventional warfare type the United States was accustomed to and comfortable with. Power and overwhelming forces were used to subdue one's foes. Still, the '60s brought an era of warfare, the most powerful nation on earth at that point in history, that they were not accustomed to, and the need for special operations groups was severely needed.

President Kennedy had the foresight for such groups and was the driving force. By 1962, a guerrilla warfare unit was born to be dubbed SEALs, an acronym for "Sea, Air, and Land," an elite group of men specialized in a wide variety of skills used in guerilla counter-guerrilla operations.

The SEALs were badly needed in the growing war in South East Asia. Their training would come from several

Army schools, which would prepare them for Special Forces techniques, evasion, and escape. These schools would also teach them the art of jungle warfare, unconventional warfare equipment, clandestine operations, including UDT (Underwater Demolition Teams), reconnaissance, sabotage, and general guerrilla warfare ambushes and counter ambushes, as well as raiding techniques.

They were to conduct covert operations on restricted waters, rivers, and canals. They were to covertly enter the enemies' shipping harbors and destroy their ships and harbors, facilities, bridges, and railway lines in any maritime area of operation and riverine environment.

In 1966, the Navy SEALs went into action in Viet Nam. Their presence "in Country" had existed in 1961. The brainchild of the Kennedy administration to use the Army and the Navy elite groups to conduct the same kind of warfare that the "Cong" used.

Brian arrived in Viet Nam in January 1968, was attached to Detachment Bravo, and went to work almost instantly in the Mekong Delta region of the Rung Sat. This area could be considered the most challenging topography in all of Viet Nam. First, its low lands were virtually impenetrable with giant mangroves consisting of twisted roots and close-growing tight packs of Nipa Palms. Then as one went inland from the hundreds of tiny tributaries of the mighty Mekong itself, it turned into double canopy forests that could and did hide the activities of the notorious Viet Cong. Then you had the noted U-Minh forest on the southern tip of Viet Nam extending onto the Western side along the Gulf of Thailand and the famous water trail of the Sihanouk, the communist supply route by sea into the eastern shores of South Viet Nam. It also connected the notorious inland route of the Ho Chi Minh Trail on the southeastern Cambodian and the South Viet Nam borders.

The Viet Cong were masters at water transportation with their famous junks, more commonly known in Viet Nam as sampans. But, for the most part, the indigenous inhabitants of the Rung Sat area were all just simple rice farmers, fishermen, and woodcutters.

Vincent and Brian had been in the Great Lakes shipping business for fifteen years and were doing exceptionally well.

As Brian arrived back at his home, the evening put him sitting on his lakeside home's large back rock patio, which he had designed himself. It made the living room face the lake with a walled glass doorway onto a thirty by twenty-foot very private area of the split level of his home.

Here he sipped on one of his favorite scotches, 21-year-old Glenfiddich single malt, and smoked his favorite brand of cigars, the 50 X 7" Macanudo. It was a tranquil evening with clear skies, and he did enjoy the area's openness, away from the big city lights and the noise. In addition, his success enabled him to enjoy the comforts of owning a home away from all the city life. Brian enjoyed leaning back in his lounge chair and looking up at the starry skies. Even with his financial success and the hard-core business world he usually had to exist in, his days were spent running two significant businesses out of his main office. As a result, Brian was a hands-on person and his evenings and nights were often in one of his hotel suites in one of the many cities spanning the length of the United States.

The quirky thing about Brian O'Francis and James O'Francis was they liked the same things. Brian had always been able to afford the things that Jim liked.

It was not until James P. moved west that he could indulge himself in the finer scotches and Irish whiskeys and cigars and just sit out under the stars, enjoying the night air and the open, clear Montana sky.

James P. was not fond of any city. He had nothing against any of them. He did not like crowds and the fast pace it took to survive. But, on the other hand, Brian had no problems with city life. It was money to him. But it was nice to be alone out in the rural area, especially from spring through the early fall, before it turned cold.

Only a select few people had the number to his home phone (he always turned his business cell phone off when he wanted extreme privacy), and one of them was Vincent Spadalini. The phone rang, and Brian slowly reached over, lifted the phone, saw who it was, and pushed talk.

"O'Francis here, talk to me."

"Brian, its Vince. Sorry to disturb you on this fine evening, old friend, and I know you are in the area of peacefulness enjoying the evening."

Brian laughed. "You got that right! So what's up?"

"I wanted to know your plans beyond our meeting tomorrow for the rest of the week."

"I have a meeting in Houston, ahh, let me think, ahh, Wednesday afternoon, ohh, around three, I think. Hell, I'll have to call Clara and double-check. Why?"

"Well, would it be possible for you to cancel the meeting?"

"Possible, yes, it depends on why."

"I would like you to meet someone...ahh, someone I think...you will want to meet. Although, I am not sure, considering all that I have learned."

A rather unusual long moment of silence occurred on the phone.

"Vincent, you are being somewhat vague with me here... I mean, just how important is this person? Is it business or something else? What is this person's name?"

"Well, let's say that I think it would be worth your time."

Brian laughed again. "Shit, I don't know; my time comes at a high price Vince."

Then more laughter by both men.

"Well, mine too. But check and see if you can postpone the meeting until Friday if your schedule allows it. I'll tell you more tomorrow after we handle this deal we are working on."

"Look, Vince, I have to meet with the hotel management tomorrow afternoon at one, so let's make it about five, back at your office."

"Good enough, we'll have dinner together."

"Okay, I'll see what I can do about Houston. No promises, you understand. Why the two-day delay? I mean, Vince, shit man, is this that important?"

"I really think so."

"Okay."

Brian hung the phone up and began to ponder why Vince felt it was so crucial to meet this mysterious, unknown person that he would not reveal his name or why the meeting was so important. Anybody else, he would have said no, but knowing Vincent, he felt it had to be something extraordinary, or he would not have asked.

The O'Francis Home Life

Patrick O'Francis had a challenging time during his freshmen and sophomore years in high school. Teachers that did not like his father would not cut him a break and gave him a difficult time with their attitude and "childish" remarks toward him in class. His math teacher refused to provide Patrick with two points in his algebra one class, which he struggled with, and Patrick failed the course. His cousin, Nico, who had the same teacher, but he would give Nico extra points to pass the course.

Jim and Dawn did not make an issue out of the matter, as they knew if Patrick had worked, he could have made an average grade or above in any given course. The problem was not his intelligence. It was with Nicodemus. Patrick was becoming resentful of him, and instead of Patrick influencing him, Nico was influencing Patrick in his work habits. Nico worked the teachers, conned them, and was good at it. Patrick did not have the "gift" to con his way through his courses. Patrick did not have the city "street" savvy like his cousin.

Jim stayed on both boys hard and pushed for them to do better. Jim had lots of problems with Nicodemus in trying to get him on the "right" road to success, not through drugs on the street, stealing from someone, taking someone's auto to make a living, or the pimping for some young girl he owned. He had lots to learn and was reluctant to accept any advice from his uncle. Nicodemus wanted to be the "bad-ass" street tough guy of Honsburg and often displayed his attitude toward his uncle, but with great care.

On one of these evenings, Nico decided that he would challenge his uncle to a physical confrontation.

"Uncle "O" are you going to work out tonight?"

"Yes, in about an hour. Why?"

"Well," then he paused. Patrick sat across the living room, just shaking his head from side to side to say, "No, you are making a mistake. You really don't want to do this."

"Ahhh... I think I can take you."

Jim smiled as his favorite show, Star Trek, returned from a commercial. "I see. "Nico," let us talk about that after Star Trek is over." Jim then turned his attention to his show, where Jean Luc finished his negotiations on the Klingon planet for Lt. Worf to regain the honor and dignity of his family name. Commercial, again. James O'Francis asked Nico how he wanted to do the sparring match.

"Okay, tell you what, Nico, let me go through my routine, and when I am done, I will let you get loose, and then we can do it any way you would like."

James O'Francis retired to his workout room. Nico seemed excited about the chance to do his uncle in. Jim spent thirty minutes going through his stretches and a few katas. Then, he returned to the living room and informed Nico that the room was all his. Nicodemus spent five minutes getting ready. Finally, Patrick came into the living room and told his dad that Nico was ready.

"So soon?" Jim asked his son.

"Hey, it's Nico, dad. What can I say?"

"Okay, Uncle O., the rules are that I can do any street moves I like, and if I can kick your ass, you will not hold it against me, right?"

"That is correct, Nico.

"Now... I can hit you in the face, right?" he stated with a great deal of confidence.

"Absolutely. You may do whatever street moves it takes. You have my word I will not hold anything against you. Nor will I get mad at you."

Patrick was standing at the far end of the family room, a fourteen-foot by thirty-foot open area, basically designed for Jim to do his katas and for the boys to play "house hoops" and general "horseplay."

Patrick had tried to warn Nico in the five minutes Nico had prepared himself for his forth-coming match to render his uncle a real city street ass kicking.

Nico, you are crazy. No way, I am telling you," Patrick warned his cousin.

But Nico did not hear Patrick's words. He was the badass from Detroit's streets, and he could take an older man in his mid-forties.

"Okay, Uncle O., I am ready."

Then he took his street fighting stance, bouncing around, fists up, a poke here, a jab there, going for his uncle's face. Jim would parry his blows and step aside in each attempt, giving him every opportunity to strike his mark. Jim was making him feel like the "bad-ass" he thought he was, proving his "manhood," getting the anger out of his system, taking it out on the authoritarian figure in his present life.

Over and over, he attempted to hurt his uncle, and on several attempts, Jim would give him a little taste of a counter-strike to his mid-section, with a medium amount of power, just enough to let him know that his old uncle could hit his mark.

Finally, after several minutes of vigorous sparring and several open hand slaps to the face to let Nico know he could be touched with a fist if he wanted, which would have hurt much worse than a light slap to the jaws.

With redness on both cheeks, Nico became mad and began swinging wildly. Jim put him on the floor with a few throws, as Nico was off-balance in his attack.

On one of his more aggressive charges toward Jim, he used the heel of his right hand as he parried Nico's right lead, stepping toward him, striking him on the forehead, pushing him as he stepped through, sending him to the floor yet again.

Nico was up quickly, making him even angrier, never understanding what his uncle could have done to his face if he had intended to hurt him instead of trying to teach him a lesson. However, Nico being Nico, began running his street mouth in a manner that was not respectful of any guardian. Especially one who had taken him in and was doing everything he could to get him on the right side of the legal system.

Jim recognized he was still just a teenager, and O'Francis kept that in mind, but enough was enough. Nico struck violently at Jim. He simply sidestepped to his left and leaned his upper body to his left to avoid the thrush of the young teen, and with the back of his right fist, he struck Nico hard in his right kidney area, sending him to the floor crying out in pain. Then Jim moved quickly just as his nephew rolled over on his back, arching, and holding his right back with his hand.

James Patrick O'Francis went down on his right knee, and putting his right hand gently around his throat, he whispered in his ear.

"Look, Mister Bad-ass from the streets of Detroit, you are all mine now. Think of what I could do to you in your current position! Remember this, Nico. *Never,* ever start a fight! You just do not know what the other person may know, and the next time the other person will not let you off without hurting you. You will bleed; trust me on this one, I know! Nico, you do not have to prove you are anything to anybody! Just be you. Your street shit just does not work one on one. It never has! It is and most likely will always be a group, a gang, doing some person in. Forget the gang shit. It will get you nowhere! Trust your dear old Uncle on this one. Please listen to me. I will not lead you in the wrong direction. Your street shit is not worth the price you will have to pay. I will not lie to you."

Then as Jim looked him in his tear-filled eyes, he saw a boy searching for a life. But the little voice in Jim's head told him that his nephew would not find the good life he wanted. The moments he looked at his nephew so close he could feel his breath on his face, Jim feared that he would not be able to save him. He could see it deep in his eyes, but he knew he had to try. Of course, he could be wrong; it could have been just the moment. He then stood and reached out his right hand, offering to help him. Nico accepted his uncle's hand as he pulled him to his feet. Jim put his arms around him and hugged him, patting him on the back.

"Go wash your face off and let's eat some popcorn and watch a movie, okay?"

He thanked his uncle with his tear-filled eyes and wet face and sniffling, and they enjoyed the rest of the evening.

☿☿

Dawn got home after eleven from her job in the video store. Jim briefed her on what had happened to have the whole story. Then, she would be able to let her sister know, who most likely would not have approved of Jim's methods of educating her youngest son. But James P. felt that she did not know her son anymore. She had lost the once little boy with great athletic ability and great potential.

Jim would tell Dawn that night,

"She will never get him back. I do not think she understands that. I do not know if Dennis understands or not, but more so than Theresa."

Dawn sat watching television, not speaking for several minutes. Appearing to Jim, she was in deep thought.

Nico still had the street in him, and he had a bad habit of lying. I do not want Dennis and Theresa to think I am mistreating their son."

"I don't think they will," she said quickly.

"Well, I know you will be talking to Theresa this week, and I know that Nico will also. So I want them to get the real story."

"You don't think Nico will tell the truth?"

"No, I do not."

"Come on, O., he has got to know they will know if he lied."

"No, Dawn, he still believes that he can con them, and, now, I do not mean anything bad here, but I am willing to bet my nuts that he feels that he can con his mother any time he wants. And Dawn, I believe he can and will. I am sorry if that sounds bad, but that is how I feel. It is what I see in him. Dennis, well, not so easy. He still has high hopes for him, but I do not know. He has a long, long way to go. That is what dealing with the scum on the street will get you. Hell Dawn, knowing the street, and letting it control you, are two different things. Nico has let it control him for too long. I really do not know if I can make him see where he is going and what is ahead of him. It depends on just how bad he wants to regain control of himself. You see, he thinks he is in control. He just does not see. The people he was associated with have done a number on him."

"Well, you have done it for others." Dawn quickly responded in defense of Nico and her sister.

"I am aware of that. I am not saying that I will not try to get the street scum washed out of his mind and help mold him into a good person. But, to use his street smarts to his advantage, I do not mean to do illegal acts but know who and when he is being conned by someone who just wants to use him for their good. That is not what I am telling you."

"Then just what are you saying?"

Jim took a deep breath.

"I am telling you he is worse off than they realize. I think more than you realize. He is good at putting on faces and moods to please his mother and you. He is a good con person. He is all street boy, and I do not know if I can get all of that out of him. He really does not like me."

Dawn interrupted Jim, "Oh come on O., I really don't think that is true."

"No, Dawn, you are wrong. He really does not. Because I know what he is, he knows I know, and he cannot con me. That is what really angers him."

Dawn sat looking at her husband from across the room. She then softly stated. "I still think he likes you."

"Oh, I agree, in a sense, he does, and I know that, but he knows I fully understand his street instincts, and that is not all that bad. It is fine to be that way if you are on the street, but not your parents, not those who care for you. He does not care. He will do whatever. It makes no difference to him. I am telling you that is the problem. I am telling you, I do not know if I can make him understand that. He thinks that the people on the street are his friends, and they are not! He cannot see that family is most important. He thinks his street thugs are his family."

Dawn never said another word as the two watched television for another hour in silence, and then went to bed.

The Recruit

Karé Edison was a lovely slender framed five foot six, one hundred and twenty pound brunette with a natural medium brown Mediterranean skin tone, inherited from her grandfather of Greek descent. She had been raised in a small town and, upon graduation, went off to a rather prestigious college. Radford was not a large university but was located near a large city that supports a college atmosphere. It was not the largest university in the Southwestern part of Virginia. It held a relatively high academic standard and once claimed to be a single-gender college for females.

In Karés senior year, she had been raped by two men as she walked from the library to her dorm. After a very long ordeal with doctors, nurses, police, campus security, and university administrators, Karé lost.

She finished her Bachelor's with a major in Computer Science and a minor in English. She then moved to Texas, a state bigger than most western European nations. She could get lost there and find herself and a new life.

Karé entered the University of Houston and got her Master's in Computer Science with the idea of joining the

United States Army in the intelligence field. Karé bought her first handgun, found an indoor firing range, and began teaching herself how to use it.

She intended to be good at firing a handgun before entering the Army. Each time she went to the range to practice, she would picture the two men that had defiled her body. She saw the corrupt legal system that would not believe her and the high and almighty university administration that covered the incident up and pulled all the correct strings to make it go away.

Her anger burned like a glowing ember deep in her psyche, releasing a rush of adrenaline that made her blood rush through her veins like hot molting lava.

Each time she had finished her practice session, she repeated mentally to herself, hunt these animals down, and assassinate *them*.

☙❧

Jordan had been visiting a childhood friend who had moved to Missouri City, Texas, a suburb on the southernmost part of Houston. It was a short drive from her home in Freeport, Texas, and she enjoyed visiting a couple of times a year. She was to have spent a week with her friend

Awindela, a Cherokee name meaning Morning, a girlfriend she had grown up with. Awindela had gotten her Master's degree from the University of Houston in Banking Finance with an emphasis on Computer Science and now worked for a large company in Houston. She lived in Missouri City on the south side of Houston on Quail Hills Drive. Jordan used the time while Awindela was at work to shop and visit an indoor shooting range close to Awindela's home.

Jordan walked into the indoor gun range at 1000 hours in the morning, spoke briefly with the range officer, paid for the time spent using the range, and got her targets. Then, she walked past the first four shooting stalls to the fifth stall, passing the only other person in the range in the morning, a woman who was at the third stall. She placed her silver gun case on the table at the rear of the stall and opened it. It was one of four cases in which she owned and recently purchased a new handgun in which she intended to do some practicing to get the feel of the pistol.

She looked down at the pistols securely placed in each of their slots of thick gray foam. On the upper part of the case, what would be considered the lid, two fully loaded magazines for each caliber handgun, her Glock 28, .380, Walther PP 7.65 MM, and her new S&W M&P 40.

Jordan practiced once a month somewhere, mostly around her home in Quintana Beach. She started her session with her Glock, and after her first magazine, she pushed the button to her right, and the target started back toward her. All ten rounds were center mass, not more than a silver dollar in spacing.

She loaded her second magazine, placed a new target on the rail, and sent it the twenty yards from her shooting stall. She emptied the next seven rounds in the chest and the last three in the head, neatly grouped.

Jordan had drunk her regular amount of coffee that morning and needed to use the lavatory. She placed the Glock and the magazines in their proper slots in the gun case and closed it, automatically setting the combinations. Then, she turned and walked to the door leading to the ladies' lavatory. As she passed the young woman at the third stall, she heard her talking to herself.

"Damn, I will get better."

Jordan smiled and continued out the door.

When she returned, the woman was sitting at the chair located at the rear of the shooting stall. Jordan passed without speaking, and when she was about ten feet by the woman, she spoke, "Excuse me, madam."

Jordan stopped and turned. "Yes, are you talking to me?"

"Yes, ma'am. May I ask you a question?"

"Sure," Jordan stated with a smile on her face.

Still seated, the woman continued.

"Forgive me, but I looked at your target while you were gone, and I truly apologize for doing so, but how did you get so good?"

Jordan continued to smile but took a few seconds to answer the woman. "What is your name?"

The woman remained seated. "My name is Karé."

"Well, Karé, I spend a lot of time practicing at gun ranges just like this one."

"That's it? Just keep shooting?"

"Well, yes, but to be really good, you need to have a feel for shooting, and you need the correct handgun and know the proper shooting techniques."

"Is there a school you can go to and learn how to be an expert?" Karé asked.

"To become an expert, well, ahh."

"Yes," Karé answered.

"Why would you want to become an expert?" Jordan asked.

Karé cleared her throat and slowly stood, placing her stub-nose .38 caliber six-shot revolver in the small brown leather case. She zipped the case closed, took a deep breath, straightened her body, looked Jordan in the eyes, and replied with an ice-cold tone in her voice.

"I have a mission."

Karé turned and started toward the door with the case in her right hand.

Just as she opened the exit door, Jordan spoke. "Karé, how serious are you about becoming an expert? I mean a real expert."

Karé stopped with her back still to Jordan. The steel gray door still opened slightly, then she stepped back one step and let the door slowly close. She turned to face Jordan, now some twenty feet away. "Dead serious."

"Then, Karé, if you would be willing to allow me to finish my practice session, I will give you your first lesson for free. Then if you would like, we can go down the street and have lunch and talk about how serious you really are."

Failure and Success

The final year's grades were into the O'Francis house, and Nico had failed Biology. Although James P. had checked with his teacher Tim Harper, Jim had found that he failed deliberately.

A year of hard times had passed for both Nico and the O'Francis family. Nico tested the waters more than once and had been grounded more than once.

James P. felt that he had some good in him, and he could, at times, show it. But for the most part, Jim saw the bad side of Nico and knew he did not want to be saved from a world of crime.

James P.'s rule was simple: if he failed anything, he would go back to his parents or an all boys' camp for rebellious youths. So Dennis and Theresa had to make the trip to Honsburg.

A night at the dining room table would catch Nico in several lies in front of his parents. He would have to come clean as to why he had done what he had in school and several other matters of concern for Dawn and Jim that had taken place in the community, of which he was not aware his aunt and uncle were even remotely aware.

He could not handle the discipline that Jim required of him. But, on the other hand, Patrick was used to it, accepted the rules, and adhered to them.

But Nico wanted to do what Nico wanted to do: stay out late at night and come and go as he pleased, which was unacceptable under the O'Francis roof.

Nico, in his anger, finally stated that he did not want to stay in the same house with his uncle. So, the following day, he was packed and off with his parents back to the city life.

In all their efforts, Jim and Dawn had tried for two years to reach Nico and had failed. Theresa did not seem happy. Jim did not know if she was upset with their son or with Dawn and Jim. Maybe she thought that the O'Francis house rules were too stern, as she was known for giving in to the demands of her son. It did not matter to James P.— his home, his rules.

Now Nicodemus would have to deal with a life that would not lead him to the riches he thought he would get out of running with the gangs on the streets of Detroit.

In the forthcoming years, Dennis and Theresa would suffer much heartache and sleepless nights because

Nicodemus did not respect nor care about anyone other than himself.

Another Playoff

The 'Cats' made the post-season playoffs and won
their first round but now had to travel east to Salem to face
Gerald Victor High School, who had gotten a bye in the first
round as they had won their conference title. They would
place the must-talked-about and a college-bound ace on the
mound—the ninety-plus fastball pitcher who had not lost a
game in his high school career. Patrick had been kept on the
varsity team at Jim's request, as the junior varsity had
become a mockery. James O'Francis had spent many hours
with Patrick during the weekends, working his baseball skills
as he had with his oldest son. Patrick had become as smooth
and skilled a second baseman as his older brother Michael.

Tim made an unannounced stop by the O'Francis
home. His visits were rare and somewhat tense after Jim's
removal from the baseball staff.

His timing was always right for one of Dawn's super
dinners, and the polite hosts the O'Francis family was, he
was invited to stay. Tension engulfed the kitchen and dining
room throughout the dinner. Jim was trying to figure out the
reason for his unannounced visit. There was little

conversation during the meal. Jim nor Dawn had no intentions of creating any dialogue.

Out of the 'blue,' Harper asked Jim to travel with the baseball team to Salem, as they were taking cars and vans, and none belonged to the school system. That way, he could ride with him. The administration could not stop him from going with the team. He told Jim he wanted him in the dugout during the game, and O'Francis looked at Harper without a word for a long ten seconds, his mind questioning why.

"Do you think that is a wise move, Tim?"

"I think it is my move! I do not have a problem with it!" Harper slowly replied.

"You may not, but I will bet *your* ass that 'They' will have a problem with it! I know for a fact that they have eyes everywhere!"

"Look, Jim, how many damn games have any of the ass-holes ever come to? They would not walk out of the school for the home games if it were not for looks!" They had several minutes of silence as they ate, and no one else talked.

James P. spoke slowly. "Well, it would be nice. I mean... just to be in the dugout again during the game. Keep in mind, and I am telling you, that it will be reported."

Tim finished his supper, got up, and went to the paper towel rack, pulled off two sheets of paper, stuffed them into a plastic cup, took out his Red Man, and packed his left jaw with a chew of tobacco. The entire time, the room was silent.

Patrick finished his dinner and went to the living room to take in some television. Jim helped Dawn clean up the dishes and put the leftover food in the refrigerator. It had been one of her very rare days off from work. Tim, of course, was very happy he had decided to stop by because eating what Jim would have fixed was not in the same "ballpark" as Dawn's cooking, and on her days off, she made a point of cooking her family a full meal.

"So, what do you say?" Harper broke the eerie silence in the room.

And before Jim could answer, Dawn spoke, "I think you should go. I mean, look, take a day off work. Hell, they damn sure won't miss you. Hell, you know they don't care if you are there or not. They would prefer you not to be there. So I think you should go and be with your son. Something that has been denied you." Her voice was stern at the end of her statement.

Over the many years of marriage, Dawn had become more and more vocal, little by little, expressing her opinion. But, of course, her intellect and educational background were so far ahead of ninety percent of the people in the community she had to lower her conversation to the bare nothing to communicate with them.

"Okay, I will go." Then he smiled, and a warm sensation came over him as if someone had reached out and sprinkled him with some type of Irish magic diamond dust. He looked at Dawn, and she had that big beautiful beaming smile covering her face.

No one knew that when James P. had went out to his car to go home that very day, he found a note on his car window. He had gotten in the car and started it before noticing the slip of paper tucked under the wiper blade on the driver's side. He opened the door, placed one foot on the pavement, raised, and reached over the windshield to take the paper out. He opened it as he stood with one foot on the pavement and one in the car.

"You have a family! Drop the suit!"

James P. read it several times. It had been typed off a computer. He knew who but also knew he could not prove it.

Hell, most people would never believe half of what he had experienced, saw, or uncovered over the years. He knew damn well they would not believe this was a note from the

Bales-Finkel connection. He also knew that 'They' had someone place it there.

He folded the paper and placed it in his briefcase.

As he sat in his car, he spoke aloud to himself. "If anyone touches my family, I will kill them!"

Game Day

Upon arrival at the field in Salem for the regional playoffs, the team walked around the field. It was an excellent flat infield that was well-groomed. The large outfield was somewhat bigger than Honsburg.

It was 325 feet down the lines. Dead center was 375 feet, a good poke for a high school player but not unheard of. The dugouts were set down in the ground, two steps down, placing the field level at one's beltline, with a chain-link wire screen in front of the face of each dugout with both ends open.

A bench ran the entire length of the dugout and a place for the bats and helmets at the home plate end. The floor of the dugout was made of concrete. The wall from the bottom of the dugout to the roof was made of concrete blocks painted in the colors of the team, which were blue and white with red trim.

As the team and coaches were dressing, Coach O'Francis felt empty inside. He was standing around saying nothing when he should be going through his ritual of putting on his uniform. But that was not the case, and he felt bitterness toward the coach that had replaced him, which was unjust as it was no fault of Coach Ziegler. He was a very good person who appeared to have a great degree of honor and integrity.

Jim O'Francis waited to follow one of his baseball superstitions, putting a chew in his mouth before going out on the baseball field.

His first step was to put in two strips of bubble gum to get it good and juicy. Then, just as he stepped foot on the green grass of the outfield, he placed his first chew of tobacco, mixing it with his bubble gum.

☿☿

Earlier that year, as Jim was preparing to call a game at Harriette High School, the catcher for Harriette asked Jim why he mixed bubble gum with chewing tobacco. He told the young catcher as he watched in astonishment.

"Well, it makes it taste better, and the bubble gum helps hold the tobacco together."

The catcher just stood and watched, saying nothing as O'Francis finished packing his jaw with the tobacco.

"Are you ready to get this game underway?" Jim asked him, smiling and putting his mask over his face. Then, before the catcher could answer, Jim continued, "You know you have the best spot on the field. This game cannot be played without you. That is just how important you are."

The young catcher beamed with pride, and with a smile as broad as the Mississippi river, he stated, "Then let's get it going."

The Honsburg players went to the right field area and got into their traditional circle. They went through their stretching routine and then broke out into a long line matching up with whomever they liked to warm up their arms. The catcher and pitchers were at one end of the line of players, something Jim had incorporated and was still intact.

The coaches were out among the players, and Jim watched in the dugout. The three managers had gotten all the equipment ready and stood alongside him. Jim felt a million miles away, and his look reflected the hollow feeling he had. He wanted to be with 'his' battery, getting them ready. Ten minutes, throwing, getting arms, shoulders, and back loose, had passed, and Tim Harper walked toward the dugout as Jim watched him approach.

"Coach O'Francis, go get the battery ready."

He stated it without the slightest question in his tone of voice. It was as if Jim was still in uniform. Harper took out his third chew of the day and walked over to the water jug. He would go through many more before the game was over, which was his nature. Jim had not moved. Tim rinsed his mouth out and saw that Jim had not moved. Tim repeated himself as he knew that Jim was hard of hearing. Coach O'Francis walked over to Harper.

"Are you sure this is a good idea?"

Tim gave him one of his looks. The look never did affect Jim.

"What about Andy?" O'Francis stated.

Then with a more stern tone in his voice, "Coach O'Francis, I want you to get the battery ready. Please."

Tim Harper and Jim O'Francis' eyes were locked. "Okay, consider it done."

It would be the first time he would be doing 'his' job in three seasons. It would also be the first time he would be doing it without a uniform.

But it was okay with Coach O'Francis, a term of endearment the players still referred to him as something he was very much aware of, that really 'ate' at the administration and some powerful political people, trivial as it was. They hated people to refer to him as Coach. In addition, his youngest son was now wearing his father's uniform. Patrick had requested that he wear his dad's number long before the season had begun, and Tim Harper made sure that he received it. On one of the rare games he attended during the regular season when Jim first saw the number 7 on Patrick, a warm feeling went through him, and goose bumps covered his entire body as a lump emerged in his throat and tears filled his eyes.

As he began his walk toward the pitcher and catcher, O'Francis' heart pounded hard. It was an instant good feeling that started at the top of his head and rolled down the entire length of his body like a great shock wave extending out from an atomic explosion. He had a bounce in his steps as he walked toward them. His attire was not what he would have wanted, black and tan Dockers shoes, no socks, jeans, and a collared three-button pullover black shirt. He walked down the long line of players tossing to one another and came to the end of the line, placing his left hand on Shane Mitchell's right shoulder.

Shane was born to be a catcher. Jim had coached him in the last year of his senior league days. He had been a hard person to control because of his temper and would get so mad at himself that one would think he would have a stroke as red as his face would get. But, Shane had listened and learned, and now he was in his senior year of varsity baseball and had come a long way as a catcher. O'Francis was very proud of him, as he knew that he had worked very hard to get where he was. Shane would, over the years Jim had been away from the team, come to Coach O'Francis and seek advice on the techniques of catching and would receive it.

He stood five feet eleven and weighed one hundred and ninety pounds, all solid muscle. He smiled as he raised his hand, "Hi, Coach." Jim motioned for Malcolm Jennings to come with O'Francis and Mitchell as Malcolm jogged up to the two already walking to the bullpen. Jim told them he was going to get them ready for the game. That part of the job had not been turned over to Andy in the past three seasons. Shane spoke. "Great!"

Then Malcolm spoke. "Great, Coach."

"I know I am not dressed for the occasion, men, but..."

Shane interrupted. "That's okay, Coach; we're just happy you are here."

Malcolm was commonly referred to as 'Moose.' Most people did not know the nickname was an Algonquian word that meant 'to strip away.'

"So, what do you think, Coach?" Malcolm stated.

Jim spit. "I think you are going to pitch a great game! I think we are going to win! I think we will hit their ace!"

One could sense the excitement in both young men, and Coach O'Francis intended to motivate them even more before the game was over. He had a rare chance to coach again, and he would do his usual encouraging pep talks to individuals as the game went on. Jim squatted behind Shane as 'Moose' got ready. He tracked the ball movement, telling Shane what pitch he wanted 'Moose' to throw.

He worked them slowly as they had a lot of time before game time. Jim would walk from the catcher to the pitcher, talk to them, build on their confidence, and remind them of the little things it took to win a big game. After returning from Malcolm to Shane, Jim placed himself in the batter's box to give Malcolm a body to throw to. Shane looked up at O'Francis.

"Coach, are you going to call the pitches for us?"

"I do not know that, Shane. That depends on what Coach Harper wants and what I am allowed to do in the dugout."

Malcolm began his final warm-up by firing four fastballs down the middle.

"Move him to the outside, Shane." Coach O'Francis said as he still stood in the batter's box to give Malcolm a better idea of where to pitch the ball, a better look at where the ball was traveling, seeing how much movement was on his fastball. After that, O'Francis would take a normal batting stance.

"Fastball?" Shane asked.

"Yes." And three pitches were on the corner thigh high.

"Now inside, Coach?"

Jim looked down and smiled. "Yes, then I will switch to the left side." They worked the right and left sides of the plate with his fastballs and then went through his breaking pitches in the same manner.

"You're ready." Coach O'Francis told 'Moose.'

Shane and O'Francis walked to the bullpen mound.

"Coach," Malcolm looked at O'Francis with a concerned look on his face, "Are you going to call the pitches for us?"

Jim spit again and looked down at the mound, raking some dirt off the pitching rubber. "I do not know."

They both started to speak, and then Shane continued as 'Moose' stopped. "I'll talk to Coach Harper if you want me to."

"Yes, I will too, Coach. Could you call the pitches for us? It makes it a lot easier for us."

"We will see. How do you feel, 'Moose?'"

"I feel great." He stated with excitement.

"Just remember, believe in yourself! You know we will not get all the pitches, and Shane, the umpire will miss some, so do not get down! That happens. And never, I mean, never say anything to the ump. If I get to call the pitches, and if the ump misses the corner, nod yes. If it was a strike, you can tell."

"Okay, Coach."

"Moose, you block out everything, do not listen to the noise! You must have complete concentration today, no matter what the call is. And if they get a hit, or even a home run, do not worry about it. That, too, will happen. Hell, guys, that happens to the pros. Just keep telling yourself that you are the best that ever walked to the mound and that you are going to throw strikes. Keep telling yourself that you are the best that ever squatted behind the plate! I do not care how much news coverage this other pitcher has gotten. You are as good as he is, and do not forget it! Concentrate on where to throw the ball. Think of nothing else. Shane, hold the mitt steady...do not forget to frame each pitch. Do not move your arm, only your wrist. Got it?"

"I will, Coach, I will!" came the response from the battery.

While O'Francis was getting the battery ready, Andy Ziegler was getting the infield and outfield ready. Jim had informed Tim that Malcolm was prepared and was looking good. Coach Ziegler had come into the dugout and gathered with Harper and Teddy to look over the lineup. Jim had walked to the other end of the dugout when Tim looked around.

"O'Francis, what are you doing? Get over here!"

O'Francis walked back to where the three coaches were. "Well, I..."

Tim cut him off quickly, "Bull, you're still a part of this team as far as I am concerned! So what do you think?" As he showed him the lineup card.

O'Francis looked over it slowly. "No DH?"

"No, Patrick would normally be the DH, but I think we may need him to pinch-hit, and that would remove him if we DH'ed him."

O'Francis looked across at Andy, who was facing him. "What do you think, Zek?"

"I like the idea myself. I mean, I have no problem with the idea of using Patrick as a pinch hitter. I mean, he has done it all year for us, and you just don't know which one of this bunch is going to be off today at the plate."

It was set, Tim liked it, and he liked how all three would have disagreed if they did not like the lineup. He was sure that Teddy and Jim would have told him if Andy had not.

As an investigative journalist, it was sometime later that I learned that Harper had stated that he would have preferred to have all three on his staff. However, the Honsburg administration and LaMar Marsey would not allow it to be. It would have made the perfect baseball staff, and Marshy was smart enough to know that. He would not let that happen, not for Tim Harper and Honsburg High School, especially not for J. Patrick O'Francis.

The fans that would typically follow the 'Cats' were in the stands by that point as the Gerald Victor Blue Devils were finishing up their infield warm-ups. Several people in the stands were not a fan of O'Francis, who had covertly assisted Damon and Finkel in getting him removed from his coaching position. Most were part of the Christian faction of the community. They spotted Jim O'Francis and made several snide remarks about him not being a coach and being in the dugout. One of the more candid and open supporters of O'Francis overheard the comments and made a point of getting up and walking two rows down to the three women and two men.

"Look, everybody knows what you have done and how you feel. I am here to tell you the majority likes for O'Francis to be where he is. But, by god, if you don't like it, why don't you get off your asses and walk down there and tell Coach Harper you don't want him in the dugout! As a matter of fact, why don't you tell Coach O'Francis to his face!"

The man stood facing O'Francis' cowardly adversaries. The people were shocked as they had been caught character assassinating O'Francis. Yet, no one moved, no one said a word.

"Yeah, just as I thought! You'll stab him behind his back, but you haven't got the guts to tell him to his face! Damn hypocrites! Hell, we lost one of the best baseball coaches this school has ever had because of people just like you!"

His anger showed, and his words were harsh. His voice had raised, and others had turned their attention to the confrontation.

Several parents clapped as he walked back to his seat, and several patted him on the shoulder and back as he passed them and re-took his seat. Then, the group of "assassins" slowly got up and moved to another part of the stands.

Dawn could not be at the game as she had to work at the video store. If Damon Bales had not unjustly rejected her as a substitute teacher, she would have. She had not seen Patrick play during the regular season and was bitter.

Dawn was more bitter not seeing her youngest son play in a regional playoff game. Her feelings would have made Bales and Marshy happy if they could have known.

During her working hours, the people she dealt with (most claiming to be good Christians) thought people like Marshy and Bales were the greatest to come along since the invention of peanut butter.

When they came into the video store, they seemed to ask probing questions, which Dawn could detect with great ease. She had, without any question, far superior intelligence than the people she had to deal with on a day in and day out basis. She would brush the probes off with a sharp response that left them dumbfounded, as they did not get her whit and sharp Italian cutting sarcasm. Her responses went so far over their heads that a Boeing 747 flying at maximum altitude could not have equaled it. The one thing that saved her day was that it was on the radio, and she could listen to the play-by-play.

Tim read the lineup, and the players got ready to face the fastball ace that had taken the mound. He looked good as Jim watched him get in his final warmup pitches before the umpire called "Play Ball." In O'Francis' mind, he was not as good as some of the pitchers the 'Cats' had faced in past years. He felt that the media had made more out of him than he really was. He appeared to have a fastball ranging in the upper eighties, and his breaking ball seemed to be only fair by O'Francis' standards. *It would make his catcher's day a difficult one*, Jim thought. Jim had been watching him in the bullpen earlier, and O'Francis had already developed an attitude about him. He was too cocky, too arrogant. He lacked discipline, and O'Francis could tell. Just something about his body language that gave it away. And O'Francis was good at reading people. Jim had become somewhat of an unofficial expert at reading people's body language, and rarely was he ever wrong.

It was game time, and the 'Cats' leadoff was a small-framed right-hander with quick feet. He was not known for his intellect but was an outstanding outfielder.

Anson threw him four straight balls, and Paul Steward was on first. O'Francis had taken note of the catcher's arm and speed of release and calculated that he could take second with Steward's speed coupled with Arson's high leg kick. But Tim did not send him. Jim knew he would have on the second pitch.

When O'Francis had been at his position in the first base coaching box, the two had been able to signal each other, forming a communication. In addition, the two coaches seem to have developed a mental connection. That allowed for confidence in each other as to strategy, which had proven to be a winning duo. The two never had a losing season in the ten years they were connected.

When Harper would question himself, it had been Jim that gave him that extra confidence to gamble. And in some cases, Jim would send a player without Harper's sign, which got him into trouble with the head coach. However, in all the years Jim O'Francis had sent a player "unauthorized" to second base, they had never had one thrown out. Jim knew his players and could read catchers like an elementary-level book. But that was not the case anymore. Zek did not have that connection with Tim, nor was he a gambler. He was not a leader and would not question Harper.

Tim Harper had expressed several times, over the years they had been apart, how he missed him on the field. Jim felt that Harper was sincere in his words on the rare occasions whenever they had crossed paths. But, deep in the recesses of his subconscious, Jim hoped he was not wrong about Harper.

Their relationship had been tainted, and he did not know if Tim even knew it. If he did, he did not show it. But Jim also knew Tim was very good at hiding his feelings. And once Jim came out of the "forest" and was able to see the "trees," he had a much different perspective of the person he had so loyally befriended.

♉♉

Bryant Milstone, the shortstop, flew out to the right fielder, and Robert Milstone, the second baseman Bart's brother, went down swinging. Mark Houston, the third baseman, hit a line drive to the second baseman, stranding

Steward at first. In the top half of the first inning, Jim was not impressed with the media's hype of Anson. But it was only the top half of the first inning, and he was only a seventeen-year-old that was as tight as a drum.

Tim looked at Jim when he walked into the dugout. There was no real need for words, *he needed him!*

O'Francis was standing alone at the far end of the dugout, and Tim walked the entire length of the dugout and stood beside him for a mere moment. "Call them!" He turned and went to the water jug at the opposite end of the dugout.

Coach O'Francis had already worked out his signals for Shane to use. Jim stepped outside to the corner of the dugout, yelling at Shane, getting his attention, and nodding his head *yes*. O'Francis could see a broad smile come across his face through his mask. Two pitches later, he threw down to second, a strong throw and 'dead on the money,' a signal to the opposing team, *"Just try me!"*

Shane walked to the mound and told 'Moose' that Coach O'Francis was calling the pitches, and 'Moose' looked over at O'Francis, nodded his head up and down, and smiled.

Shane jogged back to the plate, pulled his mask over his face, then squatted and turned his head toward Jim. So now it was Coach O'Francis who had to produce.

He called for a curveball. Most pitchers in high school start with a fastball in hopes of getting a strike, as it was crucial to get ahead of the batter. The first batter 'Moose' faced was the centerfielder.

He had not expected a breaking ball and swung late for a strike. Then, another curveball, that went into the dirt. Then a fastball off the corner for a two and one count. He called for another breaking pitch and another ball. Jim had to set the tone right away, and he knew his plan would work.

Tim never questioned him. He called for a fastball on the outside corner to the right-handed batter. He hit a looping fly ball to the right fielder for out one.

The next batter got a single. "Not to worry," Jim said, calling out to "Moose."

Their catcher batted third and grounded out to the second baseman. They had avoided the double play as a hit, and run-on was in play for the "Blue Devils." But the 'Cats' had two outs.

Now the big ace, the pitcher, the young man who could do it all for them, was at the plate.

Jim figured him for a fastball hitter and started him with a changeup. He swung so hard that he momentarily lost his balance. Then 'Moose' delivered him a sharp breaking curve that went down and away on a right-handed batter.

And it worked, as he popped up to the pitcher to end the first inning.

One of the announcers, one who knew Jim O'Francis well, stated on the air from the announcing booth, "It looks like Coach Harper has Coach O'Francis calling the pitches for the "battery." Neither announcer spoke of Jim O'Francis's removal and the break-up of Harper and O'Francis.

Dawn, listening to every word of the play-by-play, heard the statement and just smiled.

Anson collected three K's at the top of the second.

'Moose' collected his three outs with assistance from his teammates: two fly balls to the outfield and a grounder just in front of the plate. Shane was out on it quicker than a cat pouncing on a field mouse. He scooped it up, came under control, and fired a 'bullet' to his first baseman. Shane had executed the move to the chopped ball with perfection. Coach O'Francis just smiled with pride at what he saw.

The third inning saw no score, and Malcolm began to feel that he could equal the highly publicized ace.

O'Francis talked to the 'battery' in between each inning, motivating them and instilling in them that they were the best "battery" on the field.

In the fourth inning, 'Moose' got Hudson, the catcher, on a called third strike. Malcolm had run the count to a two and two. Jim had not used the change-up but once and felt that it was time. He had called out to Malcolm to focus. "Believe in yourself," and nodded at him. Hudson took the pitch; he had been fooled. His bat barrel dropped to the ground, and he stood in the box, looking back at the umpire in disbelief.

O'Francis had always feared catchers, as he felt that they were overall your best hitter. They could see the ball so much better as they saw it coming at them all the time and in many different ways. Plus, he was the leadoff man, and it was imperative to get the leadoff batter in any inning, on any level of the game. Getting the leadoff batter gave the defense the better percentage. Unlike football or basketball, baseball was all about percentages. But it was baseball, and anything could happen in the game of baseball. Since it was baseball, and it can happen, it usually did.

Anson was up and got a double, followed by their DH with a single. Finally, the 'Blue Devils' were on the scoreboard—a one-to-zip game.

O'Francis watched 'Moose' closely. He appeared to be unrattled. Then, Robbins, the DH stole second, the throw was on the line, and it was there in time, the tag was down, but the call was safe. That bothered Shane. Jim motioned for him to calm down and assured him it would work out.

Teddy screamed out from the dugout, "A little home cooking don't you think there, Mr. Umpire?"

Malcolm lost one in the dirt to Shane's right, which ricocheted off his forearm, a WP, and Robbins went to third.

Haddon, the first baseman, hit a slow roller to the second baseman, leaving Milstone no choice but to go to first base, allowing Robbins to score. Now it was a two-zip game.

'Moose' got Walls, the second baseman, to 'K' on two fastballs and a slow curve to end the inning.

The 'Cats' left two stranded on base in their half of the inning. The fifth inning saw G.V. stranding two at the corners. The 'Cats' had left two stranded also. One at first and one at second. Twice they had left runners on base.

Coach O'Francis became concerned. That was four potential scorers left on base with two innings left.

'Moose' was not tired and had been doing well. He had only thrown fifty-two pitches and matched Mr. 'Ace,' who became a little angered as the 'Cats' were making contact with his pitches. It was unfortunate that they were hit to someone, but that was all part of the game. Sometimes, baseball has 'eyes' and gets by the infielders, or the gaps, known in baseball terminology. Sometimes they don't.

In the top half of the sixth, the 'Blue Devils' went down in order, and it was time for the 'Cats' to strike, and they did. Anson walked the first batter. Then he got a called third strike out on the second batter. Teddy went off on the umpire as the ball was high and well out of the strike zone.

"Good God, Ump, he needed a ladder to reach that one! Christ, what kind of call was that?"

Jim just smiled. He knew that Ted was correct. He either missed accidentally, which can happen, or played help the 'Ace' a little. It was not the first time O'Francis witnessed such.

It was to have been a blowout. The Honsburg 'Cats' were not supposed to be in the game by this point. But, Coach O'Francis had seen it happen to them more than once in his career, so nothing surprised him. He would say nothing overt to any of the umpires. He just encouraged each batter to focus and believe in themselves.

Anson walked the next two batters and was visibly shaken. The 'Cats' had the bases loaded with one out. The 'Blue Devils' coach walked to the mound to try and calm Anson down. But, instead of listening to his coach, he bitched to him the entire time about the calls he was getting.

Jim had been right. He told himself as he observed the action at the mound. Anson was out of control, he had no discipline, and the coach did not control his 'Ace.'

As O'Francis stood at the opposite end of the dugout from the rest of the Honsburg staff, a conference began at the opposite end. Then Harper walked from his third base position to the dugout. Extremely unusual. He walked the length of the dugout to where Jim was standing.

"O'Francis, what do you think about pinch-hitting Patrick for Stockton?"

Jim looked at his ex-coaching partner and then looked around him at the other two coaches at the other end of the dugout.

"Tim, what has Paul done today?"

He spits and replies. "A walk and two Ks. But he had not been doing well lately, and he is not good in a tight situation."

Jim looked at Paul walking to the plate, the umpire was working his way to the mound, and Tim watched Jim's eyes.

"Do you think Patrick can come through for us?"

O'Francis did not hesitate. "Yes! He is an O'Francis. He will do it under pressure! Trust me, Tim, on that one!"

Tim Harper turned. Called out to 'Humper,' "Pinch-hit O'Francis." Then proceeded back to the third base coaches' box.

Teddy looked a Patrick. "You're batting."

'Hump,' who kept the books, walked about halfway to home plate and called out to Stockton to come to him. He informed him that he was being replaced and then walked to the plate umpire and changed batters.

Stockton walked into the dugout with an attitude, threw his helmet down, which was a 'no-no,' and instantly got a cold hard look from O'Francis. His overinflated ego, and usually overrunning mouth, was about to get the wrath of one H. Timothy Harper at the end of the inning.

Jim walked over to his son, who seemed calm, putting his helmet on.

"Patrick. Concentrate, and believe in yourself. I have faith in you."

Jim patted him on the butt, and he was out of the dugout and walking to the plate.

His mother was hanging on every word the play-by-play radio announcer was speaking. Then, her heart began to beat much faster when she heard her baby boy's name announced.

Jim walked to the far opposite end of the dugout from the other coaches, stepped outside, and stood with his hands crossed, resting behind his "butt."

Jim mentally requested of his spirit guide. *"My Lady, allow his abilities to surface. Give him the confidence he needs to perform."*

Then he called out to his son once more before he stepped into the batter's box. "Patrick, believe in yourself!"

Jim felt good, and he knew that his youngest son, like his older son had done many times, would come through. It was in their genes, their blood. They were O'Francis'.

Anson took his signal and delivered a strike to the sophomore right-handed batter on the outside corner. His next pitch was a strike low. Patrick had read it to be a ball.

From Jim's angle, it was low. Tim took a few steps at third and spit. Again Teddy expressed his dislike of the low call.

Dawn heard the announcer's statement.

"That one looked low.

Jim never moved from his position, his mind working.

"Watch the ball, read the pitch, follow it through to the catcher's mitt. Pull the trigger if it is close." O'Francis yelled to his son. "Read it."

Patrick took the next one low for a ball, the same place as the last pitch. Then, Anson delivered his famed fastball, and Patrick fouled it back into the stands.

Jim smiled to himself. Thinking, *"He was on that one, and he has him! He'll not get my son on this day!"*

Anson ran the count to full, and the fans were going wild.

The 'Blue Devils' coach walked to the outside of the dugout, took three steps toward the mound, stopped, then turned and walked back to the edge of the dugout.

Patrick stepped back out of the batter's box. The catcher looked up at him and then called time and jogged to the mound.

He told the other half of the batter. "He's young. Hell, man, you can blow this one by him! Now come on, let's do it!"

The catcher turned and jogged back to the plate. Patrick stepped back into the batter's box, took a couple of swings, and big Anson delivered another eighty-eight mile an hour fastball. Patrick O'Francis took his ace pitch hard to the right-field between the second baseman and first baseman with a line drive, allowing two runs to score and tying the game up.

The G.V. coach called time and went to the mound. He patted Anson on the butt and called for the relief pitcher.

As Anson went into the dugout, he threw his glove against the wall. He then kicked the helmet rack, scattering helmets over the dugout floor, sending his teammates running to the opposite end as he was throwing his childish uncontrollable temper tantrum. He then began beating his fist against the cinder block wall of the back of the dugout, cursing the young sophomore now standing on first base.

Jim clapped his hands and pointed at his son with a wide smile. Patrick clapped and pointed back at his father with a beaming smile. Tim Harper looked across at O'Francis standing at the corner of the dugout, spit, and a rare slight smile broke his face.

Dawn O'Francis bounced around the video store and out into the parking lot, screaming and yelling, dancing her Native American 'around a campfire' with joy and happiness.

An error on the left fielder from a sharp line drive gave the 'Cats' the lead. The inning ended with a K from the second basemen.

It was the seventh inning. The Honsburg 'Cats' had a one-run lead. It's do or die for the power-scoring 'Blue Devils.'

They were at the top of their order. Jim called for a change for his first pitch. The batter expected a fastball and tried to check his swing and dribbled one to the third baseman for the first out. The 'Cat's' were now two outs away from a victory over one of the most overpowering teams in the region. But, it was baseball, after all. Anyone who knew the game knew that if it could happen, it would in the game of baseball. The next batter was the third baseman, and he connected with a single to right field, putting the tying run on first. Then Malcolm slipped, and a running fastball tight inside hit the batter.

Coach O'Francis called out to 'Moose.'

"It's okay. It happens—you're Okay. Relax. Jim motioned for him to step to the back of the mound. 'Moose' was looking at Jim. Jim took a deep breath and motioned with his hands moving upward, and Jim took a deep breath. 'Moose' did the same.

"Concentrate."

'Moose' walked back to the rubber. He looked to Shane. Shane looked to Jim and then gave 'Moose' the signal.

The next batter fouled the first pitch off, a curveball. Then the strike zone shrank. Suddenly, 'Moose' could not get a strike, resulting in a walk, and the game-winning runner was on second. Jim had been in the same scenario twice before. It was like a fucking bad dream. He knew that saying anything to the umpire would do no good.

'Humper' was outraged and let the ump know it. He was right, and Jim knew it, but he had to concentrate and call the pitches. Malcolm was working like a finely oiled machine. Shane worked the plate like a pro, but the plate umpire (like many Coach O'Francis had seen before) had no ethics.

Jim called for a fastball. The batter checked his swing. Shane appealed to the first base umpire. A called strike.

Jim remembered that he had a problem with the slow-breaking curve earlier in the game and called it. The batter hit a blooper to the right field. An 'in-betweener' a 'Texas-leaguer.' Phillip, the right fielder, broke for the ball. His speed was unmatched on the team. The second baseman, Robert Milstone, broke for the ball, and the two simultaneously dove for the ball, colliding in midair, twisting each other like a pretzel. The ball went off the heel of Stockton's glove and onto the ground. The two boys lay on the ground in pain.

The ball was still in play. The first baseman ran to the ball, picking it up and throwing it home but not before two runs crossed the plate. The umpire called time, and the batter-runner held on second. Robert had injured his knee. Tim replaced him with another sophomore, Jason Justin. Stockton would have a few sore spots but remained in the game.

To add insult to injury, on the very next pitch, the plate umpire called a balk on 'Moose.' Jim knew 'Moose' had not balked. But again, Jim would not get into a verbal expression with the umpire because he knew he could not win. It would only add more problems to his already unjust tattered and stained name.

Harper remained on the surface composed. But, as usual, he would not protest the call.

'Hump' went off again and never let up for the remainder of the game. Zek, for the first time, became vocal and joined 'Humper' in their verbal barrage on the plate umpire. Jim called for a high fastball with one out, and the bases loaded for a high fastball, hoping for a pop-up. Malcolm delivered, but the batter flew out to the centerfielder, just deep enough for another run to score. The lead had switched, and the 'Blue Devils' held a five to three lead.

The center fielder, Nead, walked to the plate with a cocky strut as Jim called pitches, and Malcolm's smoothness screwed him into the ground on three straight curveballs to end a stressful inning.

The 'Cats' scored another run and left three runners stranded to end the game. Another trip to the regional playoffs, and the Honsburg 'Cats' had to come home without a victory.

☡☡

At Honsburg's downtown video store, Dawn wiped the tears from her eyes and cheeks as several customers walked in.

Joy reigned in the private homes of some of the anti-baseball power players of Honsburg, and Jim knew that Barnard Theodoric, LaMar Marshy, and Damon Bales could not have had a better ending of the school year than with the loss to the Honsburg team.

☡☡

To gaze upon the beauty of death

Dunkin Brewer retired from the school system in 1999. He continued his covert work in his semi-drug/gun dealing for his additional income. Not that he needed it to make it, as he had been well cared for by the Marshy era and being the corrupt politician he had been for many years. He had scammed the county for a sizeable amount of change.

2005 made little change in how things worked in the Reynolds County area. The investigation of Dunkin left some questions about the 'hit parade.' Dunkin was small time. However, he was a source of illegal income for the circle of corrupt Reynolds county elected and appointed members.

After some evaluations, meetings, and a few phone calls to get clearance on the matter, it was decided that he could be replaced with a better and younger operator for the area.

Dunkin's daily activities were monitored, photographed, and passed to the proper people. After that, it would be an easy job.

His lust for younger and more beautiful women made him unfaithful to his wife. Still, he thought of himself as a playboy at his age, playing the games that males and females have played, which had not changed since the time male and females were sexually attracted to each other. Whether it was your Bible-toting people that insisted the "Word" was a fact and covertly conducted their sexual games while praising their Lord and digging deep into your household income, giving it to the church. God will surely reward you for your generous contribution.

He still had an insatiable habit of drinking, although he had cut back on it to some degree over the past few years.

His Dunkin habits put him in places where a job for a professional would be made "like a walk in the park."

It was late autumn, and the mountain air was crisp in the evenings, a time for fireplaces and romance.

Dunkin left his home with a passing kiss to his wife and informed her he had to be out of town for some business. She never questioned his 'business' for all the years they had been married, although she knew he had been unfaithful for as long as she could remember. A few earlier verbal confrontations resulted in some brief bitterness, and she resolved herself to what he was and lived with it. She had a lovely home, something more than what a simple teacher's salary could have afforded, or for that matter, what a principal's salary could have in the earlier years.

LaMar had provided her husband with a well above average income through his reign, and they lived very comfortably on it and the retirement it brought. However, it did not match his income from whatever business he was involved in outside the school system. As a result, Bernice did not care anymore. There was no real romance left in their lives, just a day-in and day-out routine that she was sure many other people like her went through.

♉

Several years before Jim had retired and moved from the area, he discussed the top ten people with Paul that had been slightly part of having or had been directly involved in his hardships over the years of his simple teaching position. The list was then passed along to Joseph, who discussed it with his father-in-law and profiled what the people had done to O'Francis and his family.

Many questions were asked as to the '*whys*' of these people's actions, and no cause could be found to justify what they had done. It was Joseph's project, as it did not involve the business directly or any of the people in their business.

Brian O'Francis had been informed of '*The Project.*' And Paul knew of all the people, their comings, and their goings, and would coordinate with Joseph. What Vince did not tell Brian was the name of Joseph's friend.

Vincent and Brian had decided that Joseph could precede with his '*The Project*' but with prudence. Each of 'The Project's' steps would have to go through both men.

The next part of the overall '*Project*' was to be handled by Bruce, who would select who he wanted to help with the operation. It had been easy to put a tracking device on Dunkin's car, and they had followed him and his activities for a month. They had informed the people in the upper echelon that they would be losing one of their long-time operators. However, the business was business, and they were prepared to replace him in a matter of days of his removal as a contact/dealer/operator/mule.

The people contracted for the job picked him up a few miles from his house and followed him for over an hour to a nice hotel, where he was to meet one of the contacts he had known for many years.

Dunkin was informed that because of his loyal service for the years he had been working for the 'movers and shakers' of the drug, guns, and money business in Southwestern Virginia and often Eastern Tennessee, he was about to move to a more lucrative position. Brewer would oversee operations covering the entire five-state area.

This type of promotion was something Dunkin could not resist. His ego had been pumped to the max, and the highly seductive female accompanying the two businessmen in their meeting in early fall made it more enticing, as she had played him like a fine Stradivarius.

As he walked into the elegant dining area, it was wine and dine time.

"Good evening, Sir. May I help you?" The maitre d' spoke with a pleasant voice and a slight Italian accent.

"I am to meet Mr. Gabbana."

"Yes, Sir, if you will, just follow me." He held his hand out as he began to walk to a table in a somewhat secluded area.

As Dunkin approached the table, Nick Zileri rose from his table.

"Welcome, Dunkin. Let me introduce our business partners." He held his hand out.

"Mr. Nic Gabbana, Mr. Mario Lorenzo, and Ms. Jordan Black, whom I assume you remember."

He smiled and acknowledged that he remembered her as he was being seated. Then, the servers approached and asked Dunkin if he would like something to drink, which he did.

The business deal was discussed during the meal, and the details of what Dunkin would be doing were presented.

He accepted the offer by the end of the dinner. It was now time for Jordan to play her hand as she leaned over to Dunkin and, in a whisper, asked him to join her for a few after-dinner drinks in the lounge. As they got up from the dining table, the men all shook hands, and Jordan extended her arm for Dunkin to escort her to the lounge for their drinks.

The music was leisurely, and the mood was set as Dunkin began to feel his liquor. A small dance floor for some slow dancing made the night more of a seductive atmosphere for Dunkin. His thoughts had already turned to what he would be doing in a few hours. As they danced and their bodies rubbed against one another, Jordan used her body movement skills to get a semi-erection from her would-be seducer for the night. She began to nibble on his right ear and lick it with her tongue.

"I am quite tired. It has been a rather long day for me. Why don't you join me in my room?" It was an invitation that Dunkin had been waiting for, and he accepted eagerly.

A bottle of good champagne had been chilling in a bucket of ice. She pointed to the bottle and asked Dunkin to open it and pour them a couple of glasses to celebrate his new position in the company while she got into something more comfortable. She then turned the lights in the room down to dim.

Dunkin's heart pounded as his anticipation grew for a night of lustful sex. Jordan was among the most lustful and attractive women he had ever met.

Could this be real, he thought, *a woman like this in a room for the evening. Was this the kind of woman he would be associating with at his new level?*

She was something he had only seen in a Playboy magazine.

Her exit from the bathroom into the bedroom almost caused Dunkin to drop the bottle of champagne he was holding.

"My God," he exclaimed. He could not believe his eyes, even with his dark-rimmed glasses on. There she stood in her black, short, see-through, thigh-length negligee. She stood momentarily at the bathroom door, letting the bathroom's light to her back shine through the negligee, exposing all of her beauty for Dunkin to gaze upon. Then, in her most seductive, sexiest voice, she requested a glass of champagne. Dunkin's hands trembled as he poured the champagne into the two glasses. Finally, he turned and walked toward her. He handed her a glass, and they toasted his new job.

Jordan put her arms around his waist and pulled him to her kissing him and inserting her tongue deep into his mouth. She slowly removed his suit coat, undid his tie, took off his glasses, then began kissing him on the neck and mouth as she undid the buttons of his shirt, pulling it out of his pants.

Jordan moved him slowly toward the edge of the bed, and Dunkin lay back on it. Jordan then removed his shoes and socks and placed them on the floor at the end of the bed.

Dunkin was lying on his back, looking down at the end of the bed facing her as she stood, the dim light casting a soft glow off her smooth dark skin. Jordan removed the top of her sheer negligee, letting it drop on the floor at her feet, exposing her full naked body and firm, melon-shaped breasts. Dunkin took a deep breath, "Oh my," was all he could mutter, and then closed his eyes and awaited her voluptuous body to accompany him on the bed.

Jordan turned and walked to the dresser, opened her purse, withdrew a nine-millimeter pistol, and attached a silencer to the end. The entire time she was softly talking to Dunkin with words that sent him into a state of wonderfulness. Then, she slowly approached the end of the bed, raised her right hand, and quickly squeezed off three rounds. One to the chest, one to the throat, and one to the forehead. His body jerked only once as his eyes rolled open, only to gaze upon the beauty of death.

Jordan turned, walked to her purse, pulled out a cell phone, and dialed a number. It rang twice, and on the other end of the line, "Yes" was the response. "It is done," she replied calmly and coldly.

"Get dressed. We are on the way."

When the knock came to her door, she was clothed in a dark blue pinstriped pants suit, a beige blouse, and dark blue high heel shoes. She opened the door to greet Nic Gabbana and Nick Zileri.

"Any problems?" Nic asked.

"None." She picked up her purse and small tote bag and started out the door.

"Mario is waiting in the car in the back lot. We will see you on the plane."

The two men closed the door, put on their rubber gloves, and cleaned the room. First, they removed the body from the bed and placed it in a body bag. They then stripped the linen off the bed and replaced it with fresh new ones, including the bed cover. They then put all items in a plastic bag and began to wipe down everything in the bedroom, leaving nothing that could not have been touched. Then they cleaned the bathroom, leaving it perfectly sanitized, with no traces of anyone in the bathroom or the bedroom.

Dunkin had never registered in the hotel, and no one dealing with the hotel, restaurant, or lounge was ever introduced to him, just another face with no name for the employees. He, of course, had not told a single person where he was going or the name of any person he was to meet.

Dunkin Brewer's body was removed by the service elevator in a large laundry cart and loaded into a van at the rear of the hotel. After that, it was business as usual for anyone who might see them, just a large bundle of dirty laundry being tossed into the back of the van.

Two days later, his body was discovered five miles east of the city of Kinstown. It had been removed from the body bag and tossed off a country road in a field.

The investigation into his death posed more questions than could be answered.

It once again brought out the phone tree from people who felt that he was the victim of some ongoing conspiracy to get rid of all of them. The more they pointed the finger at James Patrick O'Francis, the more questions the investigating officers would ask them. Why this man, they would ask. Why was this O'Francis behind two murders and one missing person to date? Why would O'Francis have a reason for such acts? For so many to single out one person, there has to be a why?

Of course, none would answer that, and the officers would then ask, "Then why are you naming this O'Francis person as the one doing or behind these acts?"

Again the people making the accusations of the wrongdoings would not give the officers any answers to warrant putting an APB out on O'Francis.

None could give them a concrete answer when asked where this person was. As the investigating officers probed for answers from members of the Honsburg community, they found O'Francis was living in the Atlanta area, maybe the Boston area. Several people responded that he had moved to Dover. So he had to be in the New England states. They were unsure which one. It was just that he had talked about moving there.

Several stated that they thought he had moved to South Bend to be close to Notre Dame. There were several reports that he had moved to Ireland. The police officers dismissed the notion that the O'Francis person had anything to do with any of the events. Or if O'Francis was even alive. One report reached the desks of the investigating officers that he had died of a heart attack several years earlier, but no one know where he was at the time. As the investigating officers probed for answers, they only got the rumor mill that snaked its way through the town of Honsburg.

The Plot Thickens

It had been three weeks since the body of Dunkin Brewer had been found naked with three holes in him and a purple lily on his chest.

Roger Bushman sat at his desk reading the morning paper and sipping his coffee. His phone rang three times before he reached over with his left hand and picked it up, not taking his eyes off the article he was reading.

"Captain Bushman, may I help you?"

There was a momentary pause on the other end of the line, and a man's voice slowly spoke.

"There is a connection to the deaths of Richard Finkel, Brewer, and the disappearance of Janice Jones."

The statement got Bushman's attention.

"What?"

"You heard me."

Bushman quickly picked up a pen and asked for the names.

"With whom am I speaking?" Then the phone clicked, and it was dead.

"Hello, hello." Roger put the receiver down, rose from his chair, went to the door, opened it, walked out a few steps into the squad room, and looked around.

"Burt," referring to Burt Bass. "I need to see you in my office."

Once inside, he asked who the detective had working on the Brewer case and learned that Jason Branch was. He then called Jason into his office.

"What have you got so far on the Brewer case?"

"Not much, Captain."

"Well, what is not much?"

Captain Bushman hated to hear 'not much.' It never told him a thing.

"Well, he was from Reynolds County, Virginia. He was married with two children, who are grown up with their own families. He drank a lot and screwed around on his wife. Ahhh, let's see, ahh, he was a retired principal, ahh, that's about it."

"Have you checked his wife out?"

"Yes, Sir, I have, and she is clean. According to the coroner's time of death, she had some friends (women) over to her house, some kind of bridge group. They met each week and played cards. Her name is Bernice, and she is one of those church goers."

"Did you check with all these women she associated with?"

"Yes, Sir. They all confirmed where she was. I even checked with some of the people in the area about their card game, and they confirmed that they met every week at the same time."

"Any of the women absent from the card game that night?"

"No, Sir."

"Who is, ahh…"

Roger looked down at the notes that he quickly scribbled on his notepad. "Who is Richard Finkel?" Both detectives looked at each other, and both stated at the same time that they did not know.

The name would not have keyed a thought as the Finkel's assassination had taken place ten months earlier and some fifty miles away from the city of Kinstown.

"Okay, who is Janice Jones?" Again they had no clue what their Captain was talking about, as Jones had disappeared in Reynolds County, ninety miles away.

"I just had a phone call from someone who would not leave a name. They tell me that there was a connection between these people. He stated that the Finkel man was dead and that the Jones woman was missing. Now I want you two to get on this today. I want to know what the connection is."

The two detectives turned and began to exit the office when Branch stopped at the door.

"Oh, Captain, there was one other thing about the Brewer man."

He stood at the door. Roger waited for him to continue. When he didn't, "Okay, so what?" He barked his question as he had been in a semi-ill mood from several other cases that were not being solved.

"Well, he had a dark purple lily laying on him."

Roger paused in thought.

"Captain."

"Yeah, yeah. Look, Jason, I get the feeling that there is more to this. I don't know, but... I mean, did you not think a purple lily lying on the man's body was odd?"

"Yes, sir. I mean, we followed up on everything we could. We did not turn up anything. We asked the people around where he lived. And Captain, damn, he lived, way," as he drew out the word, "back in the mountains. I mean, there were lots of people living around there, but it's a hell-of-a long way back in the mountains. Anyway, sorry, Sir, we could not find anything connected to a purple lily."

"You checked with the local Sheriff's department?"

"Yes, Sir. Hell, we would have never found the place if we had not. They knew him and told us that he was big in politics at one time, not much else. Well, other than some of the same stuff we already had."

"You checked with the local political people? Of course, that in itself should tell us something."

"Yes. We worked with the Sheriff's department, and they helped us get what information we have."

"Which is?"

"Well, besides, he was tied into all the County politics and served as a County Supervisor for many years. So there was nothing to indicate some shady dealings going on."

"Well, he was a politician, so that would mean there was some type of shady deal somewhere. I want to find out what."

"Okay, we are on it."

"I don't know... I feel like there is something here. Re-check, find out about this person."

"Okay, we will go back and talk to some people. May turn up something."

"No, may, I want a reason for this man's death. Oh, and I want to know what the damn lily means! Also, I want you to find out about these other two people. I want to know if they were connected and how! You get their names? Find out where this, this," he looked at his notes again, "Finkel person was and where and how he died."

Then before they could take two steps, "and call the FBI and see if they have any report on a missing person in the area. They may be from the same county if there is some connection."

"Yes, sir. Got it."

"Captain, I think a purple lily means death," Jason stated, standing at the open door.

"Yeah, and just how did you come by that information?"

"I really can't remember, but I think I read it somewhere or maybe heard it on one of the Discovery channels. But I believe I am right."

Captain Branch barked, "Nevertheless, what does it mean to this person? If that is what it means, it has to be a message to someone. Who? Get on this and stay on it."

The Last Inning

It was Jim's last year with the Senior League All-Stars, and he had prepared his players well. Raymond would have to take over after Jim left the program. Raymond would do very well in the coming years as he had learned much from Coach O'Francis. He had been like a sponge absorbing everything Jim had taught the young players and the strategy for playing the game.

Raymond's son Jason and Jim's son Patrick were also playing their last All-Star games because of their age. They would now advance to the varsity level of high school. Jason (aka, simply J.J.) was behind the plate for most games. However, Jim would use him on the mound as he was a God-gifted athlete with pitching skills two years ahead of his age.

Patrick was at second, following in his big brother's footsteps. When Jason went to the mound, Jim would often put Patrick behind the plate, depending on the opponents, as he was the only person with the skills that could handle Jason's skills as a pitcher.

He would use a less skilled catcher in a less important game to give him experience at catching a good pitcher. Jim hoped the experience and instructions would develop the player into a good catcher.

At first base, Coach O'Francis had Dee Bankos, one of the best first basemen he had ever seen at that age. His stretching ability and glove work were many years ahead of his age. Next, he would have Bart Milstone, as good as they come anywhere in the country, or for that matter, most likely several counties. He was quick, had a great glove, and a strong arm as a shortstop. Then, at third, the super quiet Samuel Langley, a teacher's son, liked fishing just as well as playing baseball. Jim saw in him the ability to become a great third baseman, something the Honsburg High varsity had not had in many years.

For years, it had been the weak spot in the infield for the Honsburg Cats, but O'Francis was about to put a stop to that, working him hard at his position.

The only open critic of O'Francis from the Honsburg section was Chris Talbert, the father of Ken Talbert, who liked to play third but threw side-armed, which Jim tried to get him out of since it was a bad habit. His throws were not accurate from the third base position. Usually, the ball sailed on him on its way to first base, making it impossible for Bankos to make the play. He was slow of foot and did not have Sam's glove. Nevertheless, he had an attitude that he should start because his father volunteered his time in helping to build the high school field and his close connection to Tim Harper.

Jim and his loyal assistant Raymond saw Sam as the only choice, and Sam had earned the position.

They were to face Liberty's best, and the animosity the two teams had toward each other was evident even before the game started.

Liberty was unbeatable, so the fans often said. They had swept their opponents in their bracket with great ease. Honsburg All-Stars, on the other hand, had struggled to make it to the semi-finals, with good bunting, squeeze plays, and a couple of memorable defensive plays that caught their opponents off guard.

But now it was showtime, and Jim had prepared his team as well as anyone could have and, for that matter, much better than the greater majority of anyone could have done so in the community.

I had gone to several practices and observed Jim and Raymond prepare the fifteen and sixteen-year-old boys for a game. For Jim, it meant more than just a simple senior league game. He schooled his players on a level equal to most high school teams, with special plays of *'what ifs,'* programming them to react to situations *If* they should occur, so they would not have to think, and they had responded well to his teaching.

The fans of all the teams that had faced the Honsburg All-Stars during the 4th of July week knew of Jim's dismissal from the high school level of play. As I sat among the many fans, some anonymous to them as to who I was, or for that matter, why I was there, I often spoke of O'Francis' ability to teach the game and the enormous response he got from him his players, many were their sons.

A few were critical of him for what they perceived as too hardcore, and many *'I heard'* comments. But, be it as it may, I found over the years of research and observing on my own, the teams that he coached won the greater percentage of the games they played. In many of our conversations over the years, Jim had taught me that it was all about percentages in baseball.

I never told Jim that I had been attending many of his games, both in his league play and the tournament play and several of his practices over three years. I did not see the need to do so. I wanted to find out for myself what the man was like, not from someone else's point of view, be it positive or negative. Although I got a lot from people sitting around me in the stands, not all conversations were about baseball or O'Francis. Some of the information I gathered proved to be correct upon further investigation. Some proved to be just what it was, gossip.

However, I told Jim I had seen a few of his tournament games. This would allow me to expound on a particular game. In addition, I would have several questions for him which allowed for lengthy conversations about the game he loved.

⚯

There was a larger-than-usual crowd at the Honsburg vs. Liberty game. Maybe it was because of the reported showdown between Coach O'Francis's team and Liberty, as the coaches for Liberty were good friends and social elites of LaMar Marshy. The game was being played on a neutral field in Fortwood.

The event reminded me of the historical first significant Civil War engagement at First Manassas. The people from Washington and the nearby towns and communities poured out to watch the day's event, bringing with them their picnic lunches, the social elites in their fancy carriages, the gentlemen with their fancy suits and top hats, with their ladies at their sides in their 'high-dollar' dresses and big southern Antebellum hats.

I watched as the people poured into the ballpark and the social elites gathered in their groups. They position themselves away from the 'common' folk as if they would contract some contagious disease if they were to rub shoulders with them—especially several African Americans from the Dante area who knew the name O'Francis.

I learned that a lot of the 'general common folk' had grown up with James O'Francis. Many were from the Fortwood and St. Pete area, had known him and his mother Catherine, and were very well-liked. So they came to watch 'him' perform his 'Irish magic' as a baseball coach, hoping that his baseball 'Irish magic,' as I overheard one such person phrase it, "Beat the shit out of Liberty's best!"

I stood at the concession stand, waiting in line to get a ballpark hot dog and a coke. I was in no hurry, listening to a group of men talk about O'Francis and his team, of which I learned they were from the town Jim had grown up in.

A man with a rugged, weathered face, Tommy Davis, spoke. "Now, boys, you know him as well as I do. He'll have them ready. I've watched him for too many years now. He should be the head baseball coach at Liberty High if the truth is known."

Then one of the men with Tommy spoke. "Shit Davis, you know that just ain't going to happen. Marshy hates O'Francis."

"Yeah, well, only because he is a damn good coach, and LaMar just thinks he is."

Then the third man in the group's company spoke as they got their hot dogs and cokes and walked away.

"O'Francis probably knows more baseball in his little finger than Marshy does in that big fat body.

I'll agree with Davis, he'll have them ready, and I'll bet Liberty doesn't blow his team out. But, if he does lose, I say it will be damn close. Ain't going to be like all the rest of the teams Liberty has played. I'm telling you guys that."

Tommy spoke in his usually southern Appalachian draw and dialect.

"Now, boys, you watch how he warms his team up and how Liberty warms up. That will tell you everything. I'll put my money on O'Francis. If his pitcher is right, he'll beat Liberty. If it's close, he'll outcoach them. You watch."

"Yeah, and if he does, ole big mouth Marshy will sit in the stands and cuss him til a fly won't land on him," another of the group stated.

"Yeah, you're right, but I'll bet you a dollar to a donut that he won't to his face," Tommy stated.

"Shitttt, Tom, ain't nobody going to take that bet, you dumb-ass."

Then they laughed as they walked out of earshot toward the right-field side of the ballpark along the first baseline.

LaMar arrived in his county-supplied, high-dollar car, and waiting for his arrival was his slug-crawling friends in the parking lot. Upon arriving, they quickly gathered around him as if they were secret service agents for some special government official.

I got a laugh out of LaMar Marshy's self-deemed importance. I could only assume that he felt very secure around his awaiting entourage, which in reality, was a joke. I would learn that none of them had a military service background and little 'back-bone' to them, other than a lot of character assassinating mouths, but no more than that.

They settled at the far corner of the stands, mid-way from the top, on the third-base side. I had positioned myself in an earshot area just above them.

Marshy spotted James O'Francis in the pre-game warm-up of his infield, and Raymond was preparing the outfield, going through their routine, which they did with great perfection. For O'Francis, it was an important part of his game plan, an intimidation factor, Jim often would tell me. And in many cases, it worked if the other team had not been equally prepared both physically and mentally, more mentally than anything else.

Marshy wasted no time in his scathing criticism about O'Francis. And somewhere during the game, making the statement, "He had better enjoy what he is doing because he will never get the chance to do it on the high school level, ever again."

A statement I would hear over and over again for several years.

The one thing that I did learn about James O'Francis and his coaching was that he ran a class program, win or lose. He and the players he coached were all class on the field, in the dugout, and as they were leaving the field.

Play Ball

Liberty started with the lead, and it appeared to all in the stands that it would be another walk in the park for the All-Stars from Liberty. However, by the fifth inning, O'Francis' all-stars had regained the lead by five to three.

It was something that most players at that age would not have done. However, O'Francis's theme was forever reminding his players, *'believe in yourself.'* Honsburg had runners on first and third with one out. The batter hit the ball to the third baseman, the runner broke for home, and the throw went to the catcher. However, the runner stopped soon as the third baseman threw the ball to the catcher and hurried back to third, preventing the double play or the out at home and no time for a play at first. This action loaded the bases for the Honsburg All-Stars.

Another one of O'Francis' *IFs* was done without thought or any game yelling or hand signals, no instructions from the dugout.

The Liberty coaches went 'nuts,' yelling and screaming at their third baseman, embarrassing and belittling him in front of a large crowd.

Then Liberty's coach called time out to talk to the pitcher and catcher.

I had watched O'Francis enough to know that the move by the runner on third was a designed play, and it had been performed with perfection.

Sam was due at the plate. He appeared as calm as an experienced senior in a high school with a state championship at stake. Jim never went to him for any special words. He just gave him his signals from third and let it go, as he had all the confidence in the world in his player at the plate.

His signals appeared to be a complicated jumble of hand signals from all parts of his body, and after he had completed his sign giving to Sam and the base runners, he really had signaled nothing, simply 'hit away.' Sam did by driving a hard line drive to the left-center, scoring two runs.

The game ended with Liberty not getting another player in scoring position in the sixth or seventh inning.

Coach O'Francis's boys did threaten with runners on base in both innings but failed to score. His infield went errorless for all seven innings, with Milstone, O'Francis, and Bankos turning two double plays in the sixth and seventh to stop any late-game rallies.

The loss was taken hard by the Liberty coaches and the players and fans. The coaches refused to shake Coach O'Francis's hand and shunned him as he approached them. I learned that the people that coached the senior league teams at Liberty, that their conduct on that day was typical of their sportsmanship if they lost.

The win was sweet for both players and coaches from Honsburg. The fans in support of Jim went home that day as 'happy campers,' and Tommy repeated himself to his two friends.

"I told you guys, he would just flat outcoach them."

Marshy left cussing James Patrick O'Francis with a great deal of hate in his words and tone in his voice, and his loyal disciples echoing his words.

Dawn, Jim, and young Patrick O'Francis, who had a three for four day at the plate, enjoyed their late ten o'clock 'Big Mac' supper, rehashing the entire game.

Knowing the game of baseball, as I do now, which I am by far no expert, I knew that Liberty had all the 'guns' to win the game with ease. If put on paper, stats-wise would have, but like the honey bee who does not know it is not supposed to be able to fly, Coach O'Francis's boys did not know they were supposed to lose. James P. called every pitch, playing the odds on every pitched ball, confident in every one of his players. Jim worked his 'Irish magic' on that warm summer evening, sending the message to all his foes both in the community of Honsburg and the rest of the county that had counted him out that he was still a winner. His supporters were reminding all, *"I told you so,"* rubbing it in and enjoying every minute.

His team fell short in their final game by four to three, denying Coach O'Francis' All-Stars boys the chance to advance to the state.

As he and I talked on a later date in the early fall, while watching a Yankees game on television, he was disappointed that they did not get to advance, but he was pleased to have prepared them for their next level up in the game of baseball.

The Violin Plays On

James Patrick was re-elected as a delegate to represent the teachers in his region on a state level. He had attended one of his teacher association meetings that had run longer than usual and adjourned shortly after eight P.M.

His now, what seemed to be, friend, Emmanuel opted for a last cup of coffee at the local 'Big Mac' to go over a few items of concern introduced in the meeting but tabled until the next meeting.

It was close to nine P.M. when they departed for their respective homes, each heading in the opposite direction. But James P. did not travel far, a matter of a few hundred yards before he turned into a small sub-division and made a few lefts and rights on a few streets, and then into a small apartment building parking lot, located in the rear of the building. There were only three visitors' spaces, and one of them was occupied. Jim pulled into the one open space on the far end of the lot, which was good for what he needed. He sat in his car for a good ten minutes in silence. He had read the second note placed on the windshield of his vehicle several times, warning of impending danger to his family if he did not drop the suit.

He put on a pair of black driving gloves, reached into the back seat, and retrieved a black Army sweater and pulled it over his head, and adjusted it to his body to fit comfortably. His blue jeans and western boots of gray with black tips made for the perfect shading for the kind of night he had to operate. He reached under the driver's seat, obtained a black full-face ski mask, and pulled it over his head. Lying at the heel of his feet was a cold, black Army .45, 1911 caliber pistol, which he placed in his belt in the center of his lower back. Reaching the overhead dome light, he switched it to the off position so it would not come on when he opened the door.

As he did so, he picked up a 24-inch hard oak piece of wood about two inches in dimension, sanded smooth and treated with a coat of polyurethane, what most law enforcement people refer to as a 'nightstick.'

The 'Tonga' was a weapon used in one of his many kata's and could bring instant death to a person or render them immobile and in a great deal of pain if one knew how to use it properly, which he worked at weekly in hopes he would perfect the skill and art. He placed it in his left hand and along his left inside arm, cradling the tip in the palm of his hand.

Moving quickly to a row of pine trees separating the parking lot from the property just to the east of the long line of pines, he wrapped himself into the lower branches of the trees and waited, concealed from the untrained eye. He waited for several minutes while the dark clouds moved to cover the full, bright, late autumn moon. Then, like the stealthness of a cat on the prowl at night, he moved across the open area of a yard to the corner of a brick house. He crouched down against a large evergreen shrub as the moon's brightness reappeared to illuminate the area like some giant spotlight. As he waited, the light from a window not more than three feet away and just overhead came on, and voices from within indicated bedtime for the couple.

Another large cluster of dark clouds turned off nature's spotlight, and only the yellow glow from the bedroom window pierced the darkness.

James P. moved to within inches of the window, rising just enough to peer into the room, seeing the man reaching over to turn off the nightstand lamp and darkness. "*Bang, you're dead!*" he thought. He squatted by the house's outer wall, patting it with his right hand. "*C-4 and a remote, you're history!*"

[211]

He then waited for ten minutes as the moon came in and out. He then reached into his sweater pocket and pulled out a blue post-it pad that, with great care, he had printed the words *'There is No Time Limit'* with his left hand. Jim was ambidextrous, and no one knew outside of his family. He pulled it off the back of the hard part of the pad where he had placed the stick-on paper and had written on it, which would leave no trace on the next sheet of post-it paper.

He gently put the post-it paper in the middle of the window, knowing that eventually it would be discovered.

Like the stealth he used to get to the house, he retraced his steps back to the tree line, then to his car, and exited the parking lot; feeling good, Jim laughed and stated aloud to no one there...

"Damon Bales, you are mine! You evil bastard! I can have you anytime I want! And I will. There is no time limit!"

What made him feel even better than the actual act was that he knew he was within a few feet of Damon, and he did not have a clue. *"How easy it could be? These stupid assholes just do not know. They think they are untouchable here in their little sanctuary, and how wrong they are!"*

His oldies radio station was playing, *"We got to get out of this place if it's the last thing we ever do."* After singing along with the song, which was a habit for Jim, although he did not know all the words more often than not. He continued to speak to himself.

"Is that ever true." And then, mentally, wondered how long his *Master* intended for him to remain among the populous? Jim loved the forests, the mountains, and the climate, but the dissembling conservative social environment had become a repulsive and distasteful place to live.

Notre Dame

It had been a while since I had talked with James P., and I had been trying to keep up with his progress in his job and his court case. I became somewhat worried about him, as he did not usually go for such a long time without at least a phone call.

So I called him and invited him to come to my home for a Saturday afternoon football game. Not just any game, as he rarely watched any other game but Notre Dame.

Since the local television station refused to show HIS Irish when playing at home, which they were supposed to, or so an NBC contract stated, like most things in our society, some type of loophole allowed them to show the SEC games upsetting Jim to no end. He had written letters to NBC and made phone calls to NBC and the television station to honor ND and NBC's contract, but no one heard, like a voice in the wilderness. As often in the course of our conversations, he referred to politicians: *I am just a voice in the wilderness.*

On the other hand, I had a satellite and was able to pick up Notre Dame home games out of Atlanta. So I invited him to spend the afternoon with me, enjoying HIS Irish, watching him and his reactions to the good and the bad plays, and his comments on the officiating.

Then I could also get answers to some unanswered questions about a few stories about his school system I had picked up and knew he would have the answers.

He would never allow me to buy the beer. Instead, it was a tradition for him to bring his own and drink at least three to four of the six-pack and eat a rather large bag of pretzels during a Notre Dame game.

I noticed that James P. never criticized the coaching staff. I asked him why. I learned more about this man I had come to admire, and I respected his honesty in his response.

He took a few minutes to answer. I had also learned over the years to wait until he responded as he collected his thoughts.

"You know, John, most people do not understand coaches. Most people who watch football have never been on the field as a coach. They do not realize that you have to make decisions based on pre-game films and strategies. You have a few seconds to call a play, both offense and defense. Sometimes they work, sometimes you get a break, and sometimes they do not. When they work, you are the greatest coach in the school's history, but when they do not, you are the worst. You are stupid! "Hell, I could do better than that!"

That is what most people will say. I have been there, and it is not easy. Then when you get on the level that the Irish play, every damn school in the country is wanting to beat your ass. Then there is Notre Dame's schedule with the greater majority of their opponents ranked in the top twenty. And I do not give a rat's ass if whoever plays Notre Dame will have one of the best damn games they have ever played. Hell, they could be, ahh, shit, say, 0 and ten, with one game left in the season, and you know what, they will play some super perfect game, either upsetting the Irish or Notre Dame just barely getting by with a win in the last seconds of the game.

It has been that way for me ever since I can remember listening to them on the radio with my mother when I was a little boy."

Then he paused for a moment, took a drink of beer, and continued.

"Okay, back to your question. You can multiply the difficult factor by a thousand with every call."

The game went well for the Notre Dame Fighting Irish that day, and James P. was happy, which was very good for me. However, Jim became withdrawn and closed-mouthed when HIS Irish would lose. But he never did lay criticism on the coaches, and after asking his sons and wife about his love for Notre Dame and posing the question if they had ever heard him lay out the coaches, they too could not ever recall blaming any coach for an Irish loss. He told me once that he had coaches he liked better than others and did not like one in particular. But even with his dislike for the coach, he just stated that he was out of his league and he should have stayed at the high school level.

Notre Dame, he would say, "Is not just any college. It is a place that 99% of the coaches in the country cannot handle, no matter how good they are. I do not care what their record is. Everything changes when a new coach takes on the helm of Notre Dame football. It is a unique place in the world and has the tradition that backs it up. You either love her or hate her. There is no in-between!"

I learned one thing: anyone who knew James P. knew where he stood on the Irish. I found many of his former students from all walks of life, from professionals to laborers that would tell me, "When the Irish play on national T.V., I think of Coach O'Francis."

Fuhrer

LaMar had been in power for four years and had been sued twice. His latest teacher at the Technical Center was Ms. Susan Arnold, the drafting and architecture teacher.

The rumor reached her that her job would be terminated in the forthcoming year.

She was an attractive woman, and LaMar had not seduced her over the years, although he had tried on several occasions.

He called her to come to his office and informed her that he would have to fight the School Board to keep the course at the center, which meant he would have to fight for her job. Again, Susan bought into his story 'hook, line, and sinker.' Once again, LaMar made his pitch to her, only this time she felt as if he would save her position, but she would have to come through for him.

On several occasions, she met him in Jefferson City over the year, giving herself freely, doing all the kinky sexual favors he desired. But she had been smart and, in the back of her mind, felt that she needed some insurance, so she obtained the copies of the register LaMar had signed at the hotel they stayed. Then, to up the insurance policy, she had a friend who followed them on multiple occasions and took pictures of them entering the hotel together. She also made covert tape recordings of conversations with LaMar in the hotel and on several occasions at dinner.

LaMar cut her course and left Susan 'naked' and 'used' when it came to 'crunch time.' But unfortunately, LaMar underestimated her intelligence, her cunningness, and she brought a suit against him for sexual harassment.

As the case progressed and the evidence mounted against LaMar, the public became more aware of the events in the case.

LaMar was good, smooth, and slick and knew how to work the court system. He agreed to settle out of court. Susan Arnold did not have to work for the rest of her natural-born life, as the settlement left her financially secure.

In all their 'wisdom,' the School Board supported LaMar, and the school's insurance covered the tab, as he knew it would.

He used the school system as if it were his company. He had extracted a large sum of money from it, not to include his regular salary, which was approaching more than any superintendent in any of the eight counties surrounding Reynolds County.

Marshy ruled without question. He covered his embarrassment so well that the vast majority of the people could not see how he was working it. A master of illusion, the sleight of hand, a magician, all the things true evil is.

As O'Francis stated once, "Evil has a way of disguising itself and making friends with the world's good, although rather stupid people, and dragging them into the abyss of darkness."

The appointed School Board was so stupid that they could not see. They never questioned anything he did or said. It was, "Yes, Mr. Marshy, whatever you think. You know best."

They did all but bow to him each time they spoke or entered the room where he was present. James P. once told me he thought mentally they did and would have physically in public if he requested it.

The Dan Logger affair was beginning to get hot as more and more people became aware of his homosexual activities with the band director at Honsburg High School.

LaMar boldly walked into Dan's office and closed the door. They were at odds with each other for five minutes, and angry words were thrown back and forth. Finally, LaMar aggressively threatened Dan's job. Dan, in his anger, walked to his desk, opened the middle drawer, and took out an envelope that had been taped under it with several sexually revealing photos of LaMar.

He was retrieving them and laying them out on his desk, pointing and tapping on the pictures, and in a hate-filled voice, he stated, "And YOU are going to FIRE me! Fuck you! YOU ARE NOT GOING TO FIRE ME!"

LaMar's face was crimson red. He turned and violently left Dan's office.

☿☿

Christmas break had arrived, and the school system ground to a halt for ten days. Marshy had been laying plans to correct a few mistakes he had made in his climb to the zenith of his oligarchical powerhouse.

He established two sets of books for his financial budget and presented them to the School Board and the public. He had been a quick learner.

LaMar had pre-arranged that on the 26th of December, the School Board building would be torched. He had provided a key for the professional arsonist to enter the lower level of the building. Not that he would have needed one, as the word professional means precisely that.

For Marshy, the cost had been pocket change compared to what he would receive. He wasted no money getting the very best, as he knew that the local 'yahoos' would never figure it was torched. He looked upon the people with utter contempt as he placed himself high above them.

By the time the fire department arrived, they could contain the blaze and keep it from spreading to other buildings.

Everything had gone as planned, and all records of any importance were destroyed, leaving no paper trails.

Dan Logger had grossly miscalculated LaMar. The other copies he had, had been stored in what he felt was a secure place in the basement of the building among all the thousands of files and old documents dating back to the very beginnings of the school system itself.

Dan's blood turned cold as he knew that Marshy would be coming after him in all his fury, as no one crossed the great LaMar Marshy.

The school system relocated its central office staff into a vacant building up the street from the ruins of the School Board office. After a short time in the temporary site, LaMar walked into Dan's office and closed the door again. Then, walking over to his desk, Dan stood.

"I told you not to fuck with me. You are through." LaMar's smile reflected his evilness as he pointed his finger at Logger. Then, he chuckled a cold, bone-chilling ,deep, hollowed laugh as he turned and walked out of the room.

Before the year was over, Dan would be forced to resign as Marshy gave him no choice. Resign or face public humiliation.

LaMar had become somewhat of an expert at embezzling money from the Reynolds County School System and by the middle of the 1990s, he had secured away well over one and a half million dollars in a Nassau bank. Money could have been used to better the students or help the employees keep pace with the rising cost of living.

But Marshy was not done. Besides his lavish salary and benefits, he continued to manipulate the budget skillfully and skim off larger chunks here and there, adding to his growing account. It was easy. His personal secretary/ bookkeeper/ CFO manager was also his longtime mistress. She, of course, was not aware of all of his other extracurricular activities, although she suspected that he had different encounters. Nevertheless, she was being taken care of, and the small price she had to pay was well worth the cost as he took great care of her and had no financial worries.

The 'master' himself orchestrated the architecture for the grand central office, and every detail would have to meet his approval before it was completed.

When it was completed, the 'important' people of the county praised him and glorified LaMar in the highest. He had reached a point of supreme power. No one challenged him, as he was in complete control of every aspect of the school system and had connections to the law and judicial forces in the area. Moreover, to seal all his connections, he was a loyal and righteous dissembling member of the largest organized church in the Liberty area—a cult religious protestant force to contend with in any situation.

The grand opening of the newly constructed Reynolds School System headquarters, with all the news reporters from the area present, and with the many grand speeches delivered, none was more pronounced than the great Marshy's speech. In his closing statement, LaMar Marshy referred to the Reynolds County School Board Office as Mecca—a reference to the Islamic religion and the bowing toward the holy site of Mohammed by the Muslims.

As disrespectful as it was in mockery of one of the world's most influential religions, most people in the predominantly Southern Baptist "Bible-toting" area did not understand his callous comment about Mecca.

Attorneys

Holly Donatello called Jim and asked him to come over to her office, which was not a scheduled appointment, as they had already gone through the deposition. Jim had taken it and filled half a legal pad of notes concerning the massive amounts of mendacious statements both Finkel and Bales had made and supported his notations with his factual documentation.

On his way to her office, his little voice began sending him warnings that something was not right, and as he walked into her office, he could tell, by the look on her face, that this was not going to be a 'happy day in Mudville.'

Holly informed James Patrick O'Francis that she had health problems. As a result, she would have to discontinue her services with him but gave him an option to continue with her father's firm and allow her younger brother to carry on with the case or get someone else to represent him.

For James P., his new attorney was 'wet' behind the ears. He did not have the savvy of his sister, nor was he as organized. Moreover, he had a bad habit of procrastinating on matters Jim strongly felt were essential to his case.

In the Bales/Finkel deposition, it was alleged that James P. had made a statement to his classes that Finkel had been intimately involved with a senior, gotten her pregnant, and she had his son. Jim had time and time again denied that he had made such statements in front of any of his classes. Finally, he asked Julius Donatello to investigate why Finkel had been dismissed from his previous job.

Julius did not seem to want to find out or think that it was an important matter concerning the case.

On the other hand, Jim did and, being the reconnaissance person he was, did the 'leg' work and found that he had been dismissed due to a multitude of reasons.

The affair was with a young lady of seventeen years of age. He obtained the information from a nurse and a friend of the family who was very willing to talk about the entire event. Nurse Davies did not like Richard and thought of him as abusive and coercing young girls into sex with him. Unfortunately, she was not the first to pay the embarrassing price for her youthful stupidity. She informed James P. (whom she did not know, as O'Francis had identified himself as an investigator for a law firm in a court case and did have a private investigator's license.) that the girl's parents hated Finkel so much that the father stated to several people in the tiny community of Park Lawn that if he ever saw him in the area, he would kill him.

Jim had gotten the information concerning Richard Finkel's gambling operation from the school principal where Richard Finkel had worked at that point in time of his career. Marvin Wayne Charles had been promoted to the central office, and although he preferred not to testify, he revealed that Finkel was running a numbers game through the school.

Finkel's physical abuse of a player also came from the ex-principal. Finkel had physically slapped one of his football players several times during a practice session because he was not performing up to his expectations. He had knocked his helmet off and then slapped him across the side of his head, knocking him to the ground, yelling at him even while lying on the ground with tears in his eyes, telling him what a *'piece of shit'* of a ballplayer he was.

Finkel had been named the athletic director, and Mr. Marvin Charles freely admitted that he had made a mistake. However, in the same breath defended his appointment by stating that he had only his recommendation to go by at the time and had no clue what type of person he was.

Finkel, as the AD, led to the misappropriation of athletic funds, which Marvin Charles explained he used as cash flow for his expenses.

Jim never did tell Julius that he had done the leg work nor revealed that he had a legitimate PI license. But kept insisting that he get the information, as it would make it legal, and Jim felt that it would be a bearing on the character of Richard Finkel in the case.

James P. told Julius that their defense attorney would attack his character in court, and Julius could counter-attack them with their dark side.

Julius kept insisting that it had nothing to do with the case. Jim agreed, but he felt they would try and attack him from that point as that was all they had. He could catch Finkel in a lie and establish that he could not be believed. O'Francis felt the jury would need to hear about Fenkel's character to obtain a victory. Jim became tiresome of 'it' not being critical and presented Julius and his father with a report from an anonymous source. They, of course, wanted the name of the source. Jim informed them that he would not give it to them. However, 'they' should follow up on the report to determine whether it was credible.

Time and again, the defense attorney tried to get the case dismissed, but the judge refused.

Laying the groundwork for the case was puzzling for Jim, as he did not understand the legal 'loopholes.' Instead, he dealt with logic, truth, and facts. Either you did write the letter and send it to every 'dick' in the entire area, or you did not! It was damaging to his reputation and character, or it was not! All else to James Patrick was irrelevant. But nothing in the legal system was that simple.

Julius was not forceful enough and allowed the case to drag on and on and never followed up on the damning report on Finkel. O'Francis felt that the longer the case went without getting it into court, the less chance he had of winning.

In an afternoon meeting with Julius and his father, Lucius Donatello, several months earlier, Janice Jones alleged that the FBI had investigated Jim for what was reported to the FBI as terrorist acts.

Jim laughed aloud. Julius did not, and his father had given O'Francis a cold hard look, which did not impress nor intimidate him.

James P. did not appreciate the stern look from Lucius, and he stood, and his entire demeanor changed with the blink of one's eye. His tone of voice was stone cold as he spoke, "Gentlemen, you have no idea what lengths these people will go to discredit me! I will tell you this, you do your due diligence and contact the FBI and get their report. I will review it with you and clarify whatever they have on me. Shittttt, FBI investigates me! Damn men, that would not be hard to do. Hell, they knew all about me! It will not be difficult. The FBI has my record. Shit, let's get real here. You want facts on me. If you want the truth, the reports on me, contact the CIA. They have a record on me. In my younger days, I was recruited to work for each one of the organizations! That information damn sure does not belong in this case! But, hey, you two do some real 'leg' work and get the report from both groups. And we will go from there!"

They both looked at O'Francis, astonished at what he had said.

Julius spoke slowly, "You almost went to work for them? What do you mean?"

Jim never lost the hardness on his face.

"Like I said, you get your report from these agencies. I will not go into it. As I have stated, that, gentlemen, is off the table for this case! But I will add at this point the fact that I was once in line to become an employee of these organizations that can be confirmed. Oh, and for your record, it was my choice not to go to work for them. I was cleared to go to D.C. and the 'Farm.' Jim left the room with both men standing speechless.

Time passed, and as the case went on one month after another, James P. never did see any report from either organization.

Jim did not like what he felt. Too many trips to Julius's office for nothing. Often he was not there.

He spent long hours in the woods surrounding his home pondering the events that seemed to be controlling his life. He began to question Holly's honesty, as she had been sick. She was too ill to practice but not too ill to run for the local district attorney position, which he thought would be a very stressful political job. For O'Francis, she— they— had lied!

O'Francis never said a word to any of them, as he remained polite and friendly each time he was in their presence. He was learning quickly.

Jim had been doing a lot of the paperwork for Julius, getting documentation in order, refining the words, listing events in chronological order, and typing up the effects of the events on him and his family emotionally and financially. However, he became resentful each time he had to pay money out of his family's income toward the case, as he knew that the Reynolds County School System was footing the entire legal expenses for both Bales and Finkel.

The Unbroken Seal

Brian returned to the Chicago area waiting for a meeting with someone he knew nothing about, nor was he told his name. Vincent had informed him he wanted to meet with a person but would not reveal his name, unlike his friend and business partner.

He only knew that it was crucial and that he thought he would be pleasantly surprised.

Vincent had uncovered too many plus factors over the past several months, which the time had been good in many ways, allowing him to do some research into James Patrick and Brian's past with a lot of help from Paul. For Vincent, he was sure they were connected, just too much evidence for it not to be.

The entire Spadalini family was excited about the meeting. There was still an IF they were related by blood. If it did turn out that they were not blood-related, then they could at least meet and have a conversation, as Vincent liked James Patrick and had thoughts of maybe offering him a position with his company. Joseph encouraged his father-in-law to follow up on the matter and possibly incorporate Jim into the business or even with Brian. But, of course, he was assuming that Jim even wanted to come aboard. Paul informed all of them that Jim had a mind of his own. That Jim could not be placed in a box. That he was candid and point of fact, take him or leave him.

His portfolio indicated that he was good in the management field at one time and was an excellent organizer and a stickler for details, with an uncanny ability to recall what people said. Vincent needed a person to take over some of Brian's areas he was involved in. Vincent needed someone he could trust, someone that displayed earned loyalty. There was still a lot to consider. Vincent had no idea if James Patrick would be interested in going back to work, and of course, there was Brian, who would be directly involved as it would deal with his hotels. Both knew that the person had to fit the mold, to take some of the load off of them, but that *someone* would have to be *very* special.

♉♉

It was late spring in the north, and the morning and evening temperatures were still a little nippy but warm enough for talking outdoors during the early afternoon.

Like many other Viet Nam vets, Brian had never gotten over the war, and there were times that he drifted back and recalled his youth, both the good and the bad parts of it. The ghosts of his dreams, like all veterans of any war, never went away. So during any given day, a smell, a song, or noise would key a flashback.

The contact with Paul had been made, and Jim had been contacted. Vincent had no problem with the way Jim was informed of his invitation. On the contrary, he rather liked how he operated.

It had been eight months since his last trip to Chicago, and this trip seemed to bring uneasy anticipation for Jim. He could not quite put his finger on it. He knew it was not Joseph or his father-in-law. Something else seemed to be causing his 'gut' to feel odd. It was not fear. He pondered his feelings as he made his way through his maze of airport moves and switches, again arranged by Paul.

Jim never used his name over the phone, nor had Paul used Jim's name over the phone

Brian sat on his back patio reading a book, Gai-Jin. It was one he had been meaning to read for many years and had been sitting on his bookshelf, but he never seemed to have the time just to sit and relax and read. He had spent his R & R in Japan and had, for some strange reason, one he really could never explain, not that he had to, had always liked the Japanese culture, the bad and the good parts of such a social order. He enjoyed reading about their culture.

Occasionally, he would pause and take in the fowl and animal activities on the small lake in the back of his home. Then, he would drift and recall his tours in Viet Nam, something he was very proud of and of being a Navy SEAL.

The reputation of the SEALs had become so notorious that the average VC would not face them, given a choice to fight or run. The fear of meeting the men with the green striped faces and the fear of where these illusive men of the night would strike sent bone-chilling terror through the ranks of the Viet Cong in the Delta region. The SEALs seemed to be everywhere, even snatching village chiefs and high VC officials right out of their beds in the middle of a moonless night without a sound and in their most secure and remote places.

They were like ghosts in the night, appearing and disappearing without a trace—a tribute to guerilla warfare skills and the elite Navy SEALs.

The Delta had an estimated five million people in it. The Navy had maybe two hundred SEALs in the entire area of operation. SEALs often, when on a surveillance mission (*which was their primary job: securing information to be passed along to the military's intelligence department for the large scale operations*), the SEAL teams were not to engage the enemy if at all possible. Often this was not possible, and to avoid being compromised, silencers on their weapons or using personal knives to take out the VC kept them from being compromised.

The SEALs would, of course, not always follow the orders of the '*great minds*' behind all the operations. They seemed to just do things on their own, which was the correct way if anyone outside the specially trained men who played the actual game in Viet Nam wanted to really win the war, which seemed to be a question in the minds of SEALs and Special Forces/Ranger personnel.

Maybe it was because the '*brass*' and the '*great minds*' of Washington, all the politicians, really did not want the war to end so quickly, money being the primary factor.

Somebody was making lots of money off the 'grunts' in Nam. But not the elite, the specially trained men who knew what the war was all about and did it right. Now that upset the 'proverbial apple cart' and all the real *'head dicks'* from D.C. to Nam. The elite trained would not play by THEIR rules.

On more than one occasion, from the southernmost part of the Delta to the DMZ, someone that belonged to a Special Operations Unit, be it Army or Navy, got their 'balls' in a vice because they had not 'followed THEIR orders.'

Operating on their own did not go over well with the 'Powers in control.' But true to the very nature of Guerrilla Warfare, they played the game and played it very well. Probably the only men in the entire country who knew that the idiots calling the 'shots' had no clue what Unconventional Warfare was.

Michael and Joseph once again met James P. at the airport and, in a short time, arrived at the home of Vincent Spadalini, where Jim would be a guest. Again Jim was mildly stunned, as he had figured he would be staying at Joseph's house.

The following morning, Vincent called Brian and informed him he would arrive at his place on the lake around five o'clock, still leaving Brian in the dark about who the mystery person was.

Salvatore was the driver for Vincent, and Dalmazio Rossi, Vincent's bodyguard, was on the passenger side as they rode in a four-door black BMW with Jim and Vincent in the back.

As they traveled toward Brian's home, the two backseat passengers had meaningless small talk about politics and Vincent's business. Jim was uncomfortable on the way to this unknown destination, and Vincent did most of the talking. Vincent asked Jim if he had ever considered coming out of retirement with ten minutes left in the trip.

Jim assumed he was talking about teaching and quickly responded, "I got out of the teaching business for good. I am sure there are good school systems around the country, but I do not want any part of them. One, no system will employ a person my age. Two, I do not have my Ph.D., which eliminates the college or university aspect of employment."

Vincent smiled. "Well, Jim, I was not talking about the educational profession."

Again this set Jim off his mental prepping game for whatever was about to happen. He had no response and finished the ride in silence.

As the car made its way into the lake area, Vincent ended the conversation with, "Well, I will talk to you about it at another time. We have more important things to take care of now."

The car entered a ten-foot chain-linked fence sectioned-off area, covering three acres of land right down to the lake water's edge.

The entrance was made of steel gates that rose two feet above the ten-foot stone pillars they were attached to. They were open, and Salvatore drove through the entrance and down the driveway without hesitation.

There was only one house on the property that bordered the north side of the lake, the home of Brian Keefe O'Francis. However, on both ends and on the other side of the lake, other houses were all in the six-figure and up range.

James P. knew he was dealing with people way out of his range financially, even with his windfall and investments, most likely in other ways also. The home on the lake was not your run-of-the-mill lakeside house. More like a small countryside summer getaway, in the two million and up range.

A maid of Hispanic background (attractive, small-framed body and stood no more than five feet tall) greeted them at the door, and with the welcome, Jim knew that she knew Vincent well.

"Come in, Mr. Spadalini, come in. I will tell Mr. O'Francis you are here."

James P. was stunned at hearing his family name. He looked directly at Don Spadalini. Jim had not forgotten about the conversation that had taken place several months past. Vincent turned his head slightly to the right and saw the shocked and puzzled look on Jim's face.

"No, I know where he is. We will join him on the patio. Jim, if you will join me."

He began walking through the house with Jim two steps to his right rear. Salvatore, Rossi, and Mirabella turned and went in another direction.

Brian rose from his chair as the two men stepped onto the large stone patio overlooking the lake.

"Vincent, welcome; pull up a chair and have a seat. Been waiting for you," Brian stated as he laid his book down on the table and stood.

"Ahh, had a short delay; small matter I needed to take care of before we left," Vincent said, remaining standing.

Before Brian could call Mirabella, she appeared at the door.

"Ahh, could you bring us some..." Then he paused. "Is iced tea okay, Vince? And ahh..."

For the first time, he looked directly at James Patrick O'Francis. Their eyes locked on each other. Vincent was smiling as he stood to the left of the two men. Neither one was speaking. Their eyes went from one another's heads to their feet. Their body frame was the same, their height was the same, and their facial features were so much alike it was scary. Brian had a salt and pepper mustache, and Jim had a salt and auburn one. Both men's mustaches were shaped the same, the same length. Jim's hair was grayish/white. Brian's hair was dark gray with a bit of black left. Both had their hair parted in the middle.

Vincent broke the moments of silence. "Brian, I would like you to meet James Patrick O'Francis."

The look on Mirabella's face also told the story, and one could almost read the questions on her face as she stood staring at the two men. Then, after a moment of awakeness, Brian extended his hand, and Jim took it as the two shook hands with a firm grip and momentarily held it, with their eyes locked on one another.

"It is good to meet you, Brian O'Francis," Jim responded.

"What would you like to drink?" Brian asked.

Jim smiled. "Tea will be fine."

Brian extended his hand outward toward the chair, indicating for him to have a seat. "Sit, gentlemen."

The three men took a seat around the large round glass-top table.

"Have you two had dinner yet?" Brian asked, trying not to stare at Jim.

Vincent answered, "No, we have not. Business got in the way, and we just came on up."

Mirabella brought a tray with a pitcher of iced tea and three goblet-shaped glasses. As she set them on the table, Brian asked, "What would you like for dinner? Now, Mirabella is an excellent cook and can fix anything you would like. Vince, ah Jim. Ah, may I call you Jim or..."

"Jim is fine," as he smiled.

"Do you have a preference for dinner?"

James P. sat back in his chair, his hands cupped together, resting at his waist. Vince was pouring the tea for all three.

"No, sir, I have no particular cravings."

Vincent smiled. "Ahh, Mirabella, fix us some steaks, baked potatoes, a salad, or something like that."

"Jim," Vincent said, "she is an excellent cook, which may be a gross understatement."

Mirabella smiled from ear to ear. "Well, thank you, Mr. Spadalini. That was very kind."

"Ah, Mr. O'Francis...ahh..."

"Its okay, Mirabella. It is not often that we have another O'Francis in the house." And then he laughed. "Well, hell, we have never had one, have we?" He laughed again as he looked up at Mirabella, relieving some of the light tension that seemed to be in the air.

"Is what Mr. Spadolini suggested okay for all? When you would like to eat," she said.

"It is fine, and when you get it ready, just give us a yell, okay."

Then Vincent chimed in, "Take your time. We aren't in any hurry."

Mirabella was off to the kitchen to fix the men their meal.

Brian allowed her to fix anything she liked for herself. He rarely had anyone over to his lakeside home, but Mirabella kept a fully stocked food supply.

Mirabella had worked for Brian for ten years and had been given access to his home if he was there or away on business. He preferred her to stay, but she never would, except on rare occasions, like bad weather or late-night dinner parties. She had her own room if she needed to stay over.

Her husband had left her many years earlier. She had raised her only son Rafael Angel by herself, and Brian had made sure they had money. He had employed Mirabella when Rafael was ten years old. In a short time, he was working for Mr. Brian O'Francis, maintaining the grounds around the lakeside home during the summer. Rafael also had a separate room if he needed to spend the night or several days, which often he did when he was in his late teens.

In the winter, he had him working for him in one of his hotels or clearing the snow from his rather long driveway/road that led to his home. He made sure he went to a private school, and now he was in college at the University of Chicago.

Reunion

Brian rose from his chair. "Excuse me for a moment." He returned with a humidor, placed it on the table, and opened it.

"Have a cigar. Oh, I mean, if you smoke, that is, Jim? I don't mean to be pushy. It is just that Vincent and I usually sit out here on occasions and smoke a cigar."

"Thank you. I believe I will. I also partake in a good cigar on occasions."

Then he smiled and reached for one of Brian's Cohibas. He put it under his nose and ran it from one end to another. Jim reached for the cigar cutter and clipped the end of it off. Then, reaching his left hand into his pocket and retrieving his black Zippo lighter, he toasted the end and let the flame draw up to the end of the seven-inch cigar as he puffed and got a nice glow. James P. then laid his lighter down on the table.

Brian looked at it and saw the 75th Ranger crest attached to its side as Brian continued to draw the fire from his lighter to his cigar. His eyes shifted toward where Jim was seated. His head never moved. He then tilted his head back and blew the smoke upward into the late afternoon breeze that carried it in the opposite direction of where James P. was sitting.

"A military crest, I presume?"

It took Jim a few seconds, but he caught what he was referring to.

"Yes, it was my unit's crest, the 1st of the 75th Rangers. Well, in a way. Jim reached over to the table, picked the now worn-looking lighter up, and reached it to Brian.

"I don't believe I know what this one is. But, of course, now, I was in the Navy, and if it ain't Navy, I would not know."

James P. smiled. "Well, Brian, it sure ain't Navy. Nothing personal, you understand."

"Oh, none taken," he said as he passed the lighter back to Jim. Then he took a drink of his tea.

"Army?" Brian asked, knowing it was.

"That would be a very safe bet."

He continued with the light conversation.

"Rangers, you say. Well, now, that is impressive. Would it also be a safe bet that you are a Viet Nam Veteran?"

James P. smiled and took his time answering by taking a drink of tea and slowly setting his glass down on the table.

"Yes, that too would be a very safe bet. It seems you are winning this game of Q&A poker so far."

Brian patted his ashes off into a cigar ashtray sitting in the middle of the table for all to reach.

"Well, Jim, so far, they were no brainers. I like the emblem. Here comes another 'no brainer.' The Sun represents the day, the Star the night, and the lightning bolt means striking quickly."

Vincent laughed, and then both O'Francis men laughed.

"Yes, you won another pot."

And just as quick as the laughter began, Brian asked with a smile on his face. "So, where are you from, Jim?"

Again Jim paused before he answered, but not enough to make Brian or Vincent think he did not want to answer or that he may be hiding something.

"Currently living in Georgia."

"Ah yes, a southerner." Brian put on his best deep southern drawl. "Atlanta, right?"

Jim puffed on his cigar, reached over the ashtray, and broke his ashes off.

"Not quite, Northern Georgia, the southern part of the Appalachians. You lost that one." Jim smiled. All three laughed. The atmosphere was becoming more relaxed as the three men loosened up a bit.

Jim noticed out of the corner of his eye, undetected by Vincent, that he had been watching him, his body language, and his tone of voice as he answered the seemingly meaningless questions. Despite his Intel from Paul and Joseph, Vince still had lots to learn about Jim, which left a rather large void in his knowledge concerning him. However, his one lengthy conversation with Jim did reveal parts of Jim that he liked. Vince liked what Jim was made of, his character, and his personality. He appreciated his candidness during his talk with him.

Jim did not know just how Paul and Vincent knew each other or how well. But he was very aware that there was some type of connection, which did not bother him, as he trusted Paul, and that was enough for him.

Vincent had planned a light first meeting with casual conversations on various subjects. He hoped that the two could get together the next day and get down to a more personal level.

The three had a nice dinner, some wine, a few drinks afterward, and another cigar. They departed at ten o'clock, knowing that Jim would be returned the next day to spend the afternoon and evening with Brian, maybe even stay the night.

Personal

At precisely 1000 hours, Vincent's car pulled into Brian's driveway with only Jim and Salvatore. Jim picked up his two pieces of luggage out of the trunk and thanked Salvatore. Jim was not at all sure about this part of his trip, but he was adhering to the request of Don Spadalini. He was at the mercy of people he did not know, so he figured he would play the hand he had been dealt, figuring that Paul would not have advised him to stay for the entire course, and he would talk to him after he returned to Atlanta.

Brian met Jim at the door and waved to Salvatore as he drove off down the driveway and headed back to Chicago.

"Follow me, Jim, and I will show you to your room," Brian stated.

They walked up the arched stairway and down a hallway to one of three guest rooms. It was a plush room, large, thirty by twenty-foot, with a queen-size bed done in a Western-style décor. A large picture window looked out over the lake.

"Very nice, Brian," Jim stated as he laid his garment bag on the bed. Brian walked to the walk-in closet and opened a set of double-mirrored doors.

"You may hang your clothes in here if you wish. I understand how it is when you travel. Things get wrinkled even with the best of packing. The dressers are empty. You may put your other clothes in them also if you wish."

Brian was trying to be the perfect host, and Jim could tell Brian was a little tense with Vincent and Paul's arrangements.

"When you are done, come downstairs, and we will have coffee in the dining room. Ohhh, if you drink coffee, I mean, unless you prefer something else."

Jim cut him off. "Coffee will be fine. I like coffee, drink a lot of it, probably too much."

Brian smiled. "Yes, me too. Have you had breakfast?"

"Yes."

"I'll have Mirabella fix us a small snack. Would you like anything in particular?"

"No, just whatever you would normally have is fine." The two men stood at opposite ends of the room.

"Oh shit, forgive me. Let me show you the bathroom."

He then walked to a solid wooden door that appeared to be made of light oak and opened it.

"I think you will find everything you may need, and if you need something, let me know."

"Thanks, but I think I have all I will need."

"The towels and washcloths are here," he said as he opened a full-length mirrored door opposite the wall to the shower. Then he left Jim to put his clothes up and freshen up. After hanging his two suits, four ties, and four dress shirts in the closet, he then placed his socks, three casual slacks, two pairs of jeans, and casual shirts, as well as his sweatshirts in the dresser drawers, and put his two additional pairs of dress shoes at the foot of the bed, he went to the bathroom. It was large, fifteen feet by fifteen feet, with a walk-in shower that one could have fit three people in. It had two sinks and two full-length mirrors. It had to be specially made, Jim thought, as they opened, swinging to the left and right, revealing large and small bath towels and washcloths, enough for several people for a week, using a new one each day.

Jim noted a shelf with several new toothbrushes in sealed wrappers. There are three different kinds of toothpaste, two new razors and refills, and one electric razor. In addition, there were several bars of soap in their boxes and three different types of shampoo, all very neatly arranged. He noted that the house, what he had seen of it, was spotlessly clean and appeared to have everything in a particular place.

Brian O'Francis was, it appeared, a very meticulous and clean person and was quite sure that Brian's maid kept his home in that manner.

As Jim descended the wooden staircase, Mirabella, who appeared from a room to the left of the stairs, met him.

"Mr. O'Francis, Mr. O'Francis is waiting for you in the breakfast nook."

Jim followed her across the living room to a separate room with all windows arch-shaped from the ceiling to the floor that took up the entire corner of the west end of the house. A single swinging door led directly into the kitchen to the rear of the room, where she disappeared as soon as Jim entered the room.

Brian rose. "Have a seat." A coffee pot and two cups were on the thick octagon glass table.

"Thanks."

"Do you take anything in your coffee?"

"No, black."

Brian smiled. "Me, too." Then Brian poured two cups.

"Mirabella will have us some Danish out in a few minutes. I asked her to fix us shrimp salad and garlic bread for lunch. I hope that will do?"

Jim was taking a drink of coffee and set it down. Then stated, "Oh, that is more than enough. Hell, a simple bologna sandwich would have been fine with me."

Brian laughed. "Well, me too, but I leave the food part to Mirabella when I have a guest. Here by myself, sandwiches and "junk" food are all I eat during the day. I usually have a light breakfast and then a good dinner. Hell, I really do not have much time to eat at all."

That left an opening for Jim. "What do you do, Brian? If you do not mind me asking."

"No, No, don't mind at all. I own and operate hotels. I am also in the Lake Shipping business with Vincent."

Jim's eyebrows went up as he was impressed.

"So, Jim, what do you do for an occupation?"

"I am a retired high school teacher. Actually, for several years now. Not quite as impressive as the business world you two are in, but I was able to survive through it all."

"I take that to mean that you had difficulties?"

Jim had a half laugh as he took another drink of his coffee and reached for the pot. "May I?"

"Sure, help yourself. And if we run out, we'll make some more. Or I should say, Mirabella will. I am not allowed in the kitchen when she is here." And then Brian laughed.

"Are you married, Jim?"

"Yes. And no. I am a widow. I was married and still am to the most wonderful woman. But unfortunately, she died several years ago. Her name is Dawn Christine, and I have a son named Michael, thirty-eight, and Patrick, who would have been thirty-three this coming year. How about yourself?"

"No, never been married. And let me inject here. I am sorry for the losses in your family. As for me, I do not think I will get married, a little late at my age, and I have no desire for a permanent companion. It is not for everyone you know."

Mirabella came through the door and placed their Danish on the table and some raisin bread, butter, and butter knife.

"Will you need anything else, Mr. O'Francis?"

"I don't think so."

As the two ate their morning snack, Jim asked Brian about Mirabella, and Brian enlightened Jim on her history.

They talked about Brian's business with Vincent and his own business of hotels and where some of them were. Jim noticed that Brian appeared to be very comfortable talking to him, as well he should have, he figured, since Vincent was the one who arranged the meeting. If he could not have been trusted, he would not have been in Brian's house, much less in Vincenzo Spadalini's home.

After a tour of Brian's home, the two walked around his property. As they walked, Brian told Jim how and why he bought the property and how he had designed and overlooked the building of his home. He went into great detail about the specifics of his house, displaying great pride in it.

Jim was the one to break the ice and ask Brian specifically where he was originally from. He never said anything at the point of discovering that he also was born in the same state. Jim learned that he had family in Houston and Tulsa, Oklahoma, Texas, and California.

Jim was processing the information as fast as his brain could operate without short-circuiting. Brian talked about where he had gone to high school and college, served in the military, and the Navy, and was a SEAL.

Jim did not know a lot about SEALs other than they were specially trained in Unconventional Warfare and were part of the military's elite. He'd briefly read a few articles about them and watched one TV documentary, limiting his knowledge of the elite group.

He knew that they had carried the reputation of lavishing significant damage upon whomever they were hunting for decades. He knew that no other nation on earth could match their skills. He was well aware of the respective rivalry between SEALs, Special Forces, and Rangers as to who was the *'Baddest man in the whole damn town, or the meanest man alive, the king of the jungle jive.'* Which simply meant for the elite special operations groups, rock/roll, and count.

A few motion pictures had been made about the SEALs, but that was Hollywood, and Jim was well aware that did not tell the true story of what an actual SEAL was.

Brian had not mentioned his father's name nor elaborated on the SEALs.

Jim never asked, nor did he interrupt Brian as he was talking. He could handle just so much information at a time and figured he had more than enough time to get down to the specifics of any part of Brian Keefe O'Francis.

They ended up at the lake, where Brian had a short dock extending out into the lake, stone steps leading up to a stone patio measuring twenty by twenty feet square, several feet up from the floating dock. Black mesh iron rocking chairs and a mesh black iron table sat in the middle of the patio. They talked briefly about the weather and the lakeside view, small talk it appeared, avoiding what was nagging both men in the back of their minds.

Brian got around to asking Jim where he was born, not where he was raised. When Jim responded, he looked at Brian and saw the more than shocked look on his face. After that, each treaded lightly with their probing questions.

Jim had given a brief synopsis of where he was raised. He never named his father or mother because he was raised in his grandparent's home. It did give Brian somewhat of a false impression, but it was not a total lie. Twice they had acknowledged that they looked a lot alike. But neither time did either probe any deeper.

Brian raised forward in his chair and placed his arms on the table, cupping his hands together, looking over at James Patrick.

"Look, I want to ask you a point-blank question."

Jim stopped rocking.

"What was the name of your father?"

Jim never responded. He cleared his throat, slowly came forward, pulled his chair to the edge of the table, placed his arms on the table, cupping his hands, and then looked Brian in the eyes. "George E. O'Francis. And yours?"

Brian's eyes told him before he answered. "George E. O'Francis. What does the E. stand for? You know there could be a lot of George E. O'Francis' out there."

"Yes, you are correct about that, and I know the E. stands for Eugene."

Brian plumed backward in his chair.

"Ohhh shitttt! H-o-l-y f-u-c-k! Are we? Could we be? I mean, what... I don't think... I...?"

Jim interrupted. "Ahhh, Brian, let us take a deep breath here at this point. I do not know. I..."

Brian got up. "Look, please excuse me. I am going to the house. I need a drink!" Brian, after taking several steps, quickly turned and stated, "I drink scotch. I will bring the cigars down also. Ah, would you prefer something other than scotch to drink?"

James Patrick scooted his chair back from the table, stood, and walked to the edge of the stone patio, a few feet from Brian.

"I drink scotch! I smoke cigars! You might better bring a full bottle and a whole box of cigars! This may take a while. We may have a lot to cover or discover. This next conversation may go deep. I do not know?" Then Jim smiled.

"I think I will." Brian paused as he looked at Jim for a moment and then turned and walked up the sloping yard to the house.

As he gathered up a new bottle of Glen Livet, he picked up the humidor and started out of his den, only to be met by Mirabella.

"Brian, what is wrong? You look pale."

Brian just stood at the double doors for a moment. "Mirabella, ahh," then cleared his throat. "Ahhh, would you fix a really nice dinner for Jim and me tonight? Something exceptional."

She looked puzzled, as she would have without being asked. She could tell Brian was visibly shaken. Something she had never seen in him before in all the years she had known him. He had always been a rock, not much emotion, all business. Hard. But the man standing facing her was not the Brian O'Francis she knew.

"Is there something special you would like? Are you going to have lunch?"

Again, he had a hard time thinking about such minor things as food at the time.

"Yes, yes ah, lunch, ahh, and I really don't know about dinner, maybe a lobster dinner, with whatever you know that would go with lobster. Mirabella...I just want it to be special."

She smiled because she had already figured out the connection, a mother's instinct. Although Mirabella was two years younger than Brian, she could tell before Jim left with Vincent the day before.

"Si, Mr. O'Francis, I will make it a special dinner."

Brian took several steps by her and stopped and turned.

"Mirabella, Brian will do fine while Jim is here. It's okay. And Mirabella, I think Jim will do fine also."

Brian sounded lost at that point. Mirabella's smile covered her whole face. She beamed as if some glorious happening had just occurred to her boss. He appeared as giddy as a schoolboy, smiling all over his body. A light seemed to bream from his face. The stone-hard businessman she was so accustomed to was not present.

Jim had walked to the pier's edge and stared at the water as it moved back and forth with the light breeze.

His mind was numb, thinking about nothing because he could not figure out all the angles and was getting a headache trying.

☿ ☿

Reflections

[263]

Jim heard Brian coming and rejoined him at the table. That afternoon with the spring temperature at a warm sixty-five degrees, the two men continued to talk and learn more about each other.

By the time Mirabella informed the two half-brothers that dinner was ready, it was six-thirty, and the temperature had become cool.

The two had not noticed the time or the temperature. Jim had told him his story about what he knew of his mother and father, and Brian told him of his mother and father.

Jim learned that his father died in 1990, and Brian's mother died in 1995. Brian could not help but feel a void in Jim, growing up not knowing the same father he knew.

They learned that one had lived poor and grew up on a river and in the streets of a small town. The other, wealthy, living in a city and attending a private school.

Jim learned Brian had been told that their father had been married before and had one child, but he never told him anything other than that. Finally, he had to admit to Jim that he had forgotten about it, as he was thirteen when he had been told. He apologized to Jim at least five times and had been told five times that he need not; that was how life turned out.

At ten o'clock, Mirabella informed them that she was retiring for the evening.

By midnight, the two had finished off a liter and a half of scotch and had smoked several cigars.

The two men's conversations had become more and more personal. Jim learned that as a Navy SEAL, Brian had served in Nam, doing the same jobs as he had done, just at opposite ends of the country. It had been Brian that had broken the ice about Viet Nam.

"There were giant mangroves that produced a wide variety of insects. Mosquitoes, of course, by the billions. I think I hate that one insect more than anything. Snakes of what would seem like a fuck'en zoo, with all the different kinds *and* most very venomous! Now I damn sure don't want to forget the fuck'en blood-sucking leeches! Nor the damn spiders, where one could find, *I am sure*, the world's largest as well as variety! The entire area was a fuck'en nightmare! It had to be the most treacherous place in all of Viet Nam! Forgive me, Jim. I mean no disrespect to what you all did and where you were. Hell, I have heard horror stories about the northern sector. I am sure where you were was not a picnic. But the Delta, well, the VC, this is where they made their home. Looking back on it, and I have often looked back on it, I wish they had let the little bastards keep it! We could have found another way to stop the flow of supplies! But on the other hand, I knew there was no other way! Shit!"

He walked to the fireplace tossing another cigar stub into the low-burning fire. The scotch had begun to work on Brian, and Jim understood completely. Brian turned to face his 'new blood brother.' Jim knew he wanted to talk, and he could tell that he felt at ease talking to him, for so often, the combat veteran had no one to talk to that understood. Only another combat veteran could understand what another combat veteran had gone through. The classic comment from people who had not been there and really knew nothing about it, including all the educated medical professionals, physiologists included was, "I understand." And the usual bobbing of the head up and down as one would talk, seeking counseling, trying to make the veteran think that they understood.

"Often, we would go on surveillance missions. Of course, we were not to engage the enemy. But, unfortunately, that was not possible all the time. We were often compromised, and the result was an instant firefight. Of course, when we moved covertly into an encampment to capture or to take a few VC out and let them know that 'they' were not the rulers of the Delta, we carried silencers. When in close, we used knives to take them out. 'We' were the ghosts of the Delta. 'We' earned the reputation of being the 'ghosts with painted faces.' Brian paused momentarily, and a slight smile appeared on his face indicating that he was proud of the legendary SEALs of the Nine Dragon River Delta or Mekong Delta River area.

Looking at Jim, who had refilled both scotch glasses, and placed a couple of ice cubes in each, he thought about how they liked scotch on the rocks. Then, finally, he handed the glass to Brian.

"You know, Jim, it probably sounds like I hated being a SEAL. But that is not true!"

Brian had begun to slur some of his words and pointed his glass at Jim.

"I loved being a SEAL! I don't regret doing my time in Nam! But...goddamn it..." he sat down hard in his chair, leaned his head back, and looked up at the ceiling. "Jim, tell me, have you ever gotten over it?"

"No. Not really, Brian. I do not think in our lifetime we will ever get over it. Those ghosts will haunt us until we are dead."

"Did you like what you did?" Brian asked.

"Meaning?" Jim responded.

"I mean, did you get to the point that you liked stalking, hunting, and killing?"

That brought a very long pause in their conversation. Brian's rather lavish den seemed to succumb to the sense of danger. The moments before the hunt began. The seconds before the encounter, the heart pounds so hard the hunter can hear it in his ears. His mouth goes dry, even to the seasoned veteran. Then, the adrenaline begins to flow, that addictive substance that makes one feel they can do anything.

"Amphetamine high." Jim finally spoke. "That is what Rusty and I would call it. We got to the point where we really liked the stalking, hunting the game, and killing it. It consumed us. We competed for the most scores."

"How did you know who got the kill?"

"Ears!"

Brian rose forward in his oversized soft overstuffed chair. "Ears?"

Jim turned his glass to his mouth, finished off another double dram of scotch, then walked to the small table with the ice bucket, opened it, plucked two small ice cubes out, and dropped them into his glass. Then, he picked up the bottle of scotch that was half full and poured a two-finger into his glass. He stood with his back to Brian, swirled the scotch around a moment, and then slowly turned.

"Ears, Brian. I collected ears for each personal kill. I cannot tell you how many of the enemy that I killed. I do not think any combat vet can do that. However, I can confirm the ones I have ears from. I should say, had. I mean... I did not bring them home. Brian, I have a lot of problems with the rules of combat! We, like you, fought in a war where our idiot government officials wanted certain rules of the game to play. Of course, they were sitting in Washington, but I won't get into that. We fought an enemy that had no rules. So we were trained to fight like our enemy did. Oh, one more point, 'we' were the enemy to our enemies.

"Besides being drunk, Brian, my point is to go to places I do not like to go and talk about. My point, ahh, hell, I think I have forgotten the point. Shit! Ahhh, hell, Brian. Yes, I really liked what I did. It took me a long, long, and I mean a long time to work through all of the memories, the horrors of war.

"I put my family through some difficult times. Learning how to survive in a society with an 'I do not give a shit attitude about you and the fucking ghosts of your mind.'

"Memories in an unexpected instant, ready to 'kick open' the mental doors, exposing the scars that will not heal, the horrors that were burned into my psyche. Dragging me back into the void of violence and chaos of combat."

Brian sat and looked at Jim as he talked. Then, just as Jim had started talking, he stopped. And the room once again was filled with silence.

Brian broke the eerie silence by talking about the foods they ate during their days in 'In Country.'

After a few half-hearted laughs on the indigenous menus, the conversation trailed off again into silence as both combat veterans sat staring into the mesmerizing void of the fireplace. Minutes passed, and Jim spoke very softly as if he did not want Brian to hear what he was saying but wanted to say what was on his mind.

"There are moments still to this very day that I have the desire for that addictive substance."

Until the short oratory of Jim, Brian had been doing most of the talking, but the scotch had gotten to Jim, and he felt comfortable enough to speak his mind to Brian.

"Odd you would say that," Brian said, also in a soft voice.

Jim never responded to Brian's statement.

"I, too, desire that high, as you put it. It was an addiction. I did not think about it that way, but you are right. You did not think that it was another human you were stalking. It was the hunt, a game of sorts. But, you know Jim, we were special people, weren't we?"

Silence again permeated the room as the two sat and looked at each other as the chairs were semi-facing the fireplace. Jim sat in his chair, his arms relaxing on the arms, his drink in his left hand, his cigar smoking in his ashtray to his right.

"Yes, we were extraordinary people. We were young, and we were programmed. We were specialists in our field."

They then spoke briefly on the likes and dislikes of the press and the media during their time in 'In Country.'

Brian's scotch was getting to him, and he was rambling.

"Of course, I am sure you are aware if it were not for JFK, there would not have ever been a COIN (counter-insurgency)! No Special Forces, no Rangers, LRRPs, that is. It was us, Jim! I mean, we really knew what the war was all about!"

Holding his Cohiba toward Jim, he stated, "We were the ones that slowed down the flow of supplies, not the damn bombs!"

The two men never went to bed. Instead, they stopped drinking, went to the kitchen, made coffee, and talked about each other's lives, their parents, and their ancestral background.

Mirabella entered 'Her' kitchen at seven A.M. The two O'Francis men had stepped out on the back patio to continue their talk and drink their coffee, taking in the cool refreshing early morning air. They were almost sober by that point. The fact that they had not slept in twenty-four hours had not hit either one yet.

Mirabella walked out onto the patio. "Good morning Mr. O'Francis." And then she smiled a warm, bright smile.

"Would you two men like me to fix you something special for breakfast?"

Jim spoke as both looked at her from where they were standing and then back at each other.

"I would like a good western omelet with some toast if you do not mind?"

"And you, Brian?" Mirabella asked.

"That will be good, with a lot of bacon, please."

Mirabella turned and went to 'Her' kitchen to make what the two men requested. Brian went into the kitchen and told Mirabella they were going for a walk and for her to take her time fixing breakfast. During their walk, Jim learned about Brian's connection to Vincent and other people. In addition, he learned about Brian's men, who took care of his business for him. Jim found that he was an influential figure in the financial and business world.

Brian discovered that Jim was much like him but without wealth and connections.

"You know Brian; it was altogether different for me. I grew up in a small town." He then stopped and began to laugh. Brian was smiling but did not understand what had struck Jim funny.

As he continued to laugh, Brian looked at him. "What?"

"Have you ever heard of or listened to a singer named John Mellencamp?"

"Oh, yes, why?"

"He wrote a song a long time ago called *Small Town*. It struck a chord in me the first time I heard it, and the song suddenly came to mind."

Jim paused, and slowly his laughter faded, and the smile on his face slowly went away. "God... it really is weird what a song will do to your mind."

After a few minutes of silence as the two continued to walk, Brian looked over at Jim and stated,

"Hey...only in America."

"No, No, No, It's, *Ain't that America..*" Jim said.

"Ohhh, Yaaa, it is."

The two men laughed together. Brian had not been so relaxed since his college days when life was just fun.

"Jim, tell me, I understand we have a mutual friend down south."

They continued to walk. Jim had not responded to his question.

"Look, Jim, I am not trying to probe nor test you. Paul has known Vincent and me for some years now.

"Jim, I did not know, nor did I have a clue we were brothers. Vincent simply told me he had someone he wanted me to meet and that you knew Paul."

"Well, yes, I do know Paul. But I am not connected with him as far as his business goes. Hell, I really do not know exactly what business he is in. Well, that is not exactly true. I mean, I do know he has a PI business, but I mean, I really do not know what his background is.

He has helped me with his ability to obtain information. But, for us, that is "recon," and surveillance of some... let me put it this way, some undesirables."

They had reached the crest of the gently sloping ground that overlooked Brian's property.

"Jim, please don't take this the wrong way. I don't mean to get personal here, although we have been for the past, ahh, every how many hours it has been. I do not intend to pry into your private life. But, how are you financially?"

Jim took a long drag off his half-smoked, once a seven-inch, cigar. He blew the smoke upward into the crisp early morning air. He extended his right arm outward and held the 'stogie' as if he were examining it.

"This is a very expensive cigar. Or to me, it is!"

Brian never answered.

He stood beside his newly found brother, paused only for a moment, and continued.

"You have never wanted for much, have you? I mean, you have always been financially well off, correct?"

Brian started to speak and then paused and removed his cigar from his mouth.

"Yes, Jim, that is correct. And I am very..."

Jim cut him off in mid-sentence.

" No! You owe me no apology. Nor do you owe me any type of explanation. That is just how the cards were dealt! I had to play my hand, and you had to play yours. Now, to your question: I am not rich by any means! But at this point in my life, I am above water! However, as you now know, it has not always been that way."

They spent the entire day together, sharing everything they could with each other and learning just how much they were alike.

With different mothers, Brian's of Italian ancestry and Jim's of Scottish ancestry. However, their father's genes were dominant in both O'Francis men.

Jim learned a lot about the father he had never seen, yet he had always felt that he and his father were alike. As he would learn, he had been correct. They were, and as his beloved mother had often stated. "You're just like your damn father!"

Brian had taken on more of the Italian skin pigmentations and hair color. Jim had gotten his skin tone and hair from his Celtic mother and grandmother O'Francis. But the physical structure and their faces left no questions.

Brian was kind enough to share his pictures of his father with Jim, and there had been no question about the father and son connection. Jim kept looking at the photos of his father as if he were burning the images into his mind so as not to forget. But he had not needed to worry. He left with several pictures, compliments of his brother.

The Long Trip Home

Jim had a stop-over in Atlanta and met Paul in one of the airport cafés.

Jim did not learn how Paul came to know Brian and Vincent. But he did not care. Instead, their conversations concerning his unexpected adventure and discovery was pleasant.

His biggest concern was the fact that sooner or later, they would learn that he did not live in Georgia. However, Paul informed him that he would take care of that end of the connection in due time and that it would not be a significant problem.

"Paul, did you know that I had a brother? Well, I guess he would be considered a half-brother. I mean according to socially correct terms, that is."

"Not at first, to be completely honest with you, Jim."

He drank his coffee, and the waitress arrived, filled his cup, and looked over at Jim. "More, Sir?"

Jim just nodded yes. He looked down at his cup as she filled it to the brim.

"Jim, what are your thoughts?" Paul inquired.

"Do you know how long..." Jim paused, and Paul finished his sentence,

"You looked for your father."

"Yes. Well, no, I really do not. But I made the connection between you two in 1997. So I really came about it by accident. I had not really given it a lot of thought, until I was sitting in Don Spadalini's den and Brian came in.

The more I looked at him, the more I made the connection. Or thought I did. I mean, damn, Jim, you two, well, it would take a blind person not to see the similarities. I never said anything to anyone. I did not know all the connections. So when I got back home, I started checking and called in a few low-cost favors, and bang, there was the connection."

"All these years, you have known that I had a brother, and you did not tell me."

"It was not my place to tell you. And besides, I did not know at the time you had or was trying to locate your father."

There were several minutes of silence, with only the sounds of the other people in the café, utensils touching the plates, and some ambient music being played in the background.

"You know Brian is a very powerful person, don't you?"

Jim did not respond. Paul sat looking at him. Finally, Jim slowly looked up from staring into his coffee cup.

"I did not. Well, I should say I really do not know. I mean, I figured. But, hell, I am not a complete idiot. I know he has and is in a very powerful financial world with very powerful and wealthy people."

"I know you're no idiot," Paul stated. "But, I think you could have fit into…" another pause as Paul carefully chose his words.

"I think you would have worked out well in the business."

"The business?" Jim asked.

"Yes," Paul stated.

Jim looked down at his watch. He had forty-five minutes before his flight left. His thoughts were that Paul seemed to be different. He seemed to look at him from a different perspective than he had. Maybe he did not. Perhaps it was just his paranoia surfacing. He knew he was in a world with people who could control people's destinies with a coin flip.

Paul did not interrupt Jim's thoughts. He knew he was doing just that: figuring, calculating, and putting together pieces of a puzzle. He had a total military mind. Even at his age, he had not lost the sharpness. Not that sixty-five was old, maybe at one time, but not now. Jim was one that planned and calculated every move, figuring the odds. That was why he knew that he would fit into the business. He knew that Vincent and Brian would see it if they got close to Jim. That is, if he would let them.

Paul could not blame him if he did not, but he also knew he was not totally wealthy and could be, with a bit of help from people like Vincent and Brian.

Jim got up without speaking and tossed ten dollars on the table.

"Let's take a walk toward the gate." He was halfway to the gate before he spoke again.

"So when will you come to see me, Paul?"

The statement took Paul by surprise, and it took several moments before he could answer. "I don't know. I guess whenever you want."

"Well, the weather is turning early this year. So spring should be getting an early start. Fishing is really good in the early spring. Why not give me a call?"

"Okay." That was all Paul could say, and then he gave him a new password, and they parted.

Jim headed to the northwest by way of the southwest, Paul headed to the northeast by way of a car, and both with a lot to think about.

The Cage

It was 7:00 A.M. when the phone started to ring in O'Neill's office. After the fifth ring, the answering machine picked up. *You have reached Blue Ridge Investigation. Leave your name and number and a short message. I will return your call.*

"This is Henry David Thoreau. Call me."

It was 10:00 A.M. when Paul walked into his office.

"Good morning Mary; you're looking bright and spiffy for a Monday morning."

Mary J. Pendergrass smiled. "Thank you, Mr. O'Neill. Your mail is on your desk, and you have had three phone calls this morning. I left the messages on your desk. Coffee?"

"Yes, please." Paul O'Neill went into his office. The answering machine was on the right corner of his desk, the light flashing. Paul sat down in his old battered chair and began opening his mail, mostly junk. Three were checks for services rendered. Mary J. came in with coffee in his favorite mug, a faded tan mug with an Irish and American flag unfurled, crossed in the center and wrapped around the sides of the mug's handle. A gift from a 'Brother.'

"Thanks, Mary. Would you put these checks in the bank for me this morning?" He signed the backs of each and handed them to her.

"Do you want me to go now, or do you need me for anything right away?"

"I'll be here for a while. You can go this morning. Oh, Mary, would you be so kind as to pick us up some breakfast while you are out? Would you please?"

"The usual?" Mary asked.

Paul smiled. "Yes, I guess. No, no, on second thought, surprise me this time." Then Paul smiled at his loyal secretary of ten years.

Mary J. turned and walked out of his office, closing the door behind her as she left.

Paul took a drink of coffee while he reached the corner of the desk and pushed play on the answering machine. "Damn, she makes good coffee," Paul spoke aloud. He swung his old chair around and placed his feet on the low windowsill, and leaned back, the chair squeaking as it went back. He enjoyed just looking out of the two corner windows down to the street below. Paul enjoyed watching the people and traffic going about their daily routines. The first message was from a female needing his services, the second an attorney who frequently required his services, and the third a voice he had not heard in some time.

"Hmmm. Now that is a pleasant surprise." He said as he once again spoke aloud. He leaned to his right and picked up the phone. He was aware that only a few people had Jim's number or knew where he was, for that matter. So it had to be important for him to call him. Paul had his number stored in his memory banks and punched in the number on the phone.

It was 7:25 A.M. in Montana. Jim was at the kitchen table eating his breakfast. He had fixed oatmeal and toast. The early spring weather on O'Brian Creek was still cool, in the upper 40s during the day, then dropping to the mid-to-low twenties at night. Snow still covered the ground, and the sun was extremely bright as it brightly illuminated the O'Francis kitchen.

The phone rang for the third time by the time he reached it on the wall on the far side of the kitchen. He looked at the caller ID. It read Blue Ridge Investigation.

"This is Thoreau. Talk to me."

"This is Longfellow.

"How goes business in the hustling, bustling, big city?" James Patrick started the conversation.

"Oh, I'm staying as busy as I want. Same old stuff; someone wants to find out who is cheating on someone. How are things in your neck of the woods?" Paul asked.

"Well, we still have a good blanket of snow on the ground, but it is getting warmer by the day, though," Jim said.

Paul laughed. "Yeah, I bet it's up to zero by now." Then he continued to chuckle.

"Oh, we're up to the upper 40's during the days. It does seem warmer when the sun is out. The reflection will just about blind you, though. Ahhh, give Mother Nature a few weeks, and she will have her green carpet covering everything," Jim said as if to defend the weather at the foothills of the Bitterroot Mountains.

Paul was well aware that Jim did not call for a friendly chat.

"So, my old friend, what can I do for you?" Paul's voice became serious.

"Can your 'cable tow' extend to Minneapolis for a brief meeting?" Jim said.

There was a short pause in the conversation as Paul took his feet off the windowsill and leaned forward in his chair, squeaking as he came forward and scooted it toward the edge of the windows. He looked down at the people coming and going on the sidewalks, entering and exiting the stores in the renovated new downtown. The 60 degree spring morning seemed to motivate people to get out and about.

"Yes. Sure. Why Minneapolis?" Paul asked.

"No real reason. I just figured it to be about halfway for the both of us. Would you not say?" Jim answered.

"Yeah, not a problem. So where and when do we meet?" Asked Paul.

"Don't know yet. I'll make the arrangements and call you back this afternoon," Jim said.

"Okay. I'll be in the office all day." Paul told Jim. Then Jim hung up without any goodbye or so long, or see you later. Paul knew him well, and although it may have bothered most people and most would have thought it rude, Paul accepted how Jim operated.

It was early Friday morning when Jim checked into the Hilton and Towers on 1001 Marquette Avenue in downtown Minneapolis 18 days after talking to Paul. Paul was due to arrive Saturday morning. James P. had reserved a room next to his. After getting settled into his room, Jim strolled out on the sidewalk of Marquette Avenue and hailed a cab, telling the driver to take him to First and Marquette. He paid the fare, got out, and walked the short distance to Riverside Park on the shores of the mighty Mississippi River. He found a park bench and took a seat. The air was a cool 50 degrees at eleven o'clock, and a mild breeze blew from the north down the river, making it feel like it was 30 degrees. Jim had dressed in jeans, light tan western boots, a blue denim shirt, and his favorite cowhide sheep-lined coat for the weather. He sat with his hands in his coat pockets, looking out at the almond-shaped island splitting the Mississippi. He watched the busy traffic on the river and the bridge leading across the river to the island. But his mind did not comprehend any of it. Instead, he was pondering what he was about to set in motion.

⚇

It was Saturday morning at 9:00 A.M. when Paul entered the hotel restaurant. There were just a few people in the room, maybe ten or twelve. He paused and scanned the room for Jim as he had received a message at the desk to meet him in the restaurant when he was settled in.

The hostess approached Paul, and before she could ask him where he would like to be seated, he informed her that he was meeting a gentleman and had located him.

Jim was in the far corner of the restaurant and had seen Paul enter. He stood and raised his arm so he could locate him. Paul thanked the hostess and made his way across the room to Jim's table.

"Good morning, Paul," O'Francis said. "Good flight?"

"Ahh, no problems, enjoyed it. Good to do a little long-distance traveling again. I think I miss it," Paul said with a smile on his face.

They had no more than sat down when the waitress arrived. "Good morning, Gentlemen. May I get you something to drink?"

"Coffee and plenty of it, please," Paul told her.

"I'll be right back." And she was off.

"So, Jim, you look like you have been keeping in shape."

"Don't look too shabby yourself, ole boy," Jim replied.

The waitress returned with a container of coffee and turned each cup over on the saucers and filled them.

"May I take your order now? Or would you like some time to look at a menu?"

Paul looked at her nametag. "Well, Carol, I think I'll have your house special."

Jim stated that he would have the same.

"Would you like to know what it is?" Carol asked.

"No, I am sure it is good," Paul stated.

"Okay, Gentlemen, it'll be a few minutes." Carol turned and was off again.

"Well, 'Brother,' why are we here in the great Viking city of Minneapolis?" Paul opened the business conversation up.

Jim took a long drink of coffee, set his cup gently down in his saucer, and looked across the table at Paul.

"I want to build a cage," Jim said with calm, an almost coldness in his voice.

Paul put his cup down. "A cage?" he asked.

"Yes, a cage, a Viet Cong cage," Jim answered with no feelings in his voice.

"I don't think I understand," Paul stated puzzled.

"Do you know anyone in the Bayous of Louisiana?" Jim continued.

Paul took another drink of coffee. He thought for a few minutes, his hands wrapped around his cup.

Jim sat in silence as Paul pondered.

Then some meaningless conversation took place between the two. Jim and Paul covered the political climate, the weather, travel, and what Jim had been doing with himself on his ranch. Then, finally, the waitress arrived with their breakfast.

"Well, that didn't take long," Jim stated.

"Well, it is easy when you order the house special," Carol answered with a friendly smile. She continued to place each plate down, telling them what they were having: "two eggs, scrambled, three pieces of bacon, three pieces of toast, and a bowl of fruit, Gentlemen. Will there be anything else?"

"No. It looks good. Just keep us filled with coffee," Jim told Carol.

She picked up the container and was off with a response of, "Yes, Sir. I'll be right back."

As the two men ate their breakfast, they continued their talk about the politics of the Nation, the weather, and Jim's buffalo ranch. Carol returned with a full container of coffee.

As soon as the men were finished, Carol took their plates away from their table. "Fresh coffee, Gentlemen," she asked pleasantly.

"Yes, if you don't mind," Paul told her.

"No problem. I'll be right back," Carol stated and took the plates and container.

Paul finally answered Jim's question. "I think I can locate a source in the swampland. Why do we need someone in the deep swamps of Louisiana?" as Paul picked up on the business end of the conversation again.

"The first thing I want is a small isolated island somewhere deep in the swamps. I want to build a cage 4 X 4 X 4 feet, top, bottom, and sides, with two inches between each pole. I want the poles to be two inches in diameter. I want the cage to be three feet off the ground. I want one bamboo mat placed on the floor of the cage. I want one slit cut measuring 2 inches high and 6 inches long set in one of the middle bottom back sections of the cage to slide a round aluminum pan into the cage. I want it built with the hardest wooden poles that can be obtained. I want it constructed with screws, not nails, so no one can escape! Can that be done?" Again, Jim stated this with coldness in his voice.

Paul looked at him for several minutes, his mind analyzing the specific request before he spoke. Then Paul stated, "James Patrick, what the hell is going down, my Brother?"

Jim did not answer right away. "Can you get what I am asking for?" Jim stated without answering Paul's question.

"Well, I'll have to make some phone calls. But, yes, I can make this happen. Now, my question is, why?" Paul picked up his cup to take another drink.

"Paul, you told me long ago that there was no time limit after a most enlightening dinner meeting. Do you remember?"

Paul looked at Jim. "Geez, do you remember everything someone tells you? I mean, that was outside the restaurant in the parking lot." Jim did not answer his question. But continued...

"I will have someone placed in it for a long time. This person will not return from the swamp. They will not be found. I want someone we can trust to provide this individual with one daily meal. I want this person to be provided with one fish, one cup of white rice, and one cup of water at each meal." Jim continued with his request. "The provider is not to have any conversations with this person. Then, after one month, I want the provider of the meals to forget where the cage is. I do not want to know the provider's name. I do not want him to know the person's name in the cage. I want this done through a series of channels and covertly."

"Damn Jim, this is a Viet Cong tactic. That is cold, you and Brian...no, sorry...none of business. My apologies." Paul stated.

"Yes, it is just that. Yes, it is cruel, cold, and sadistic. I learned. I remembered. Knowledge is power. I know what it will do to even the well-trained, experienced hardened person. Yes, some most likely would consider this action cruel. But it is not cruel enough." Jim stated. Paul was looking directly into Jim's eyes as he was speaking. There was nothing there—an empty void.

"What about the cost?" Paul asked, knowing that Jim was not wealthy. However, he knew he was not hurting for money and knew he had a brother with the finances who could handle any cost for whatever Jim wanted.

"The cost will be covered, whatever it is! You will get a check in the mail." The reply came from Jim.

"Who's the mark, Jim?" Before he could answer, Paul asked, "Have you arranged for this person to be abducted? Have you got your ass covered on this mission?"

Jim finished off yet another cup of coffee and poured a half-cup. "To answer all your questions, affirmative, and the mark is a female and a deadly enemy."

Carol brought the check, and Jim placed fifty dollars in with the bill and handed it to her.

"Keep the change." He and Paul went to the restroom and then exited the restaurant/hotel.

"Let's go for a walk, Paul," Jim said as they walked out on Marquette Avenue.

"Which way? I know you have reconned the area," Paul laughed.

"Ahhh, come on, Paul, why would you think that?"

Jim nodded his head toward the river.

"It's not far by country boys' standards. We'll walk to the great and mighty Mississippi. There is a nice park at Marquette and First Street," O'Francis stated.

At the block's end, a few hundred feet from the hotel, Paul looked at the cross street.

"Damn, this is Tenth Street. And we are going to First. So you have got to be kidding, right?" Paul stood as the light changed and people began crossing the street.

"Let's go, city boy." Jim stepped off the curb and crossed the street toward Riverside Park.

Time to Pay the Price

Janice Jones had always been incompetent at her job, but Marshy and Theodoric ensured she was well cared for. Her promotion to Reynolds County's Family Life program and under-the-table graft made for a very lucrative position. She had been able to work the weak-minded teachers like putty in her hands as she came in contact with them throughout the county with her deception and evil, manipulative methods, especially when character assassinating O'Francis.

During her tenure as an employee of Reynold's County, Jones was paid very well to do 'Master' Marshy's work among the 'flocks.'

She had retired from the corrupt life she had led for several years. It was Friday in May, and Janice visited one of her old cronies. She had just left one of her disciple's and one of her old lover's houses and pulled up to a stop sign on a back street in the subdivision of Liberty. She was only a mile away from the four-lane highway through the county. It was one-thirty when a plain white van bumped into the rear of her year-old Volvo, breaking her right rear tail light. A woman dressed in overalls, with a heating and air condition label on her left upper breast area, got out. She stood five feet six inches and weighed one hundred twenty-five pounds. She had a cap with the same label covering her black hair tied up in a ponytail sticking out of the opening at the back of the hat. Her facial complexion revealed the natural dark brown skin of a Native American.

Janice slung open her door and quickly walked back to the rear of her car. Then, Janice went into her usual mode of rapid talking, which had not changed in thirty-plus years. First, she verbally chastised the woman driver for her stupidity and poor driving. Then she began using an array of socially 'unacceptable terms' at every other breath, which she still, at the point in time, claimed that she never used.

The woman asked Janice to step to her van, and she would provide her with the insurance company, the number to call, and her name. She assured her that it would all be taken care of while being extremely apologetic, all the time humbling herself and asking forgiveness.

Janice never stopped 'jacking her jaws' the entire time they walked around the van's rear to the passenger side. The sliding panel door opened as soon as the van's passenger door opened. A mid-thirties man with a well-defined body, 'well-cut,' six-two, two hundred pounds, grabbed Jones' blouse and light dress jacket at the left breast area. He quickly pulled her toward him and hit Janice Jones square with his right fist in the mouth and nose. The impact of his large fist jolted her head back violently, splattering blood over both sides of her face.

He pulled and lifted her into the van in the same fluid motion. The woman driver of the van closed the sliding door, then reached into the passenger's side, retrieving a green wrapping paper off the seat, then closing the passenger's door. As she walked to Janice's car, putting on a pair of black tight-fitting driving gloves on her hands, she unfolded the green wrapping paper. Taking a dark purple lily out with her right hand and dropping it on the driver's seat of the Volvo. She returned to the van, got in, backed up enough to clear Janice's car, and then drove slowly away.

While the woman dropped the lily on Janice's Volvo seat, the man quickly injected Janice with ketamine.

Being in a dazed state from the 'shot to the face,' Janice was quickly unconscious on the van's floor.

There had been no other traffic in the area at the time of the accident, and the gray Volvo was left sitting at the stop sign, the motor still running, and the driver's door closed. Her once-girlfriend and part-time lover had a dentist appointment at two o'clock. As she approached the same stop sign, seeing Janice's car, she checked the vehicle. Not seeing Janice, she knew that something was wrong. She went to her car, picked up her cell phone, and called the police, who arrived in minutes.

John Frederick O'Donovan sat and read his Tuesday newspaper as he ate his brunch, and on the front page, the headlines read EX-TEACHER MISSING. The story included loose-ended details, how a full investigation was taking place by the local police and the State police.

He quickly got up and went to his phone, dialing the number to the newspaper office, requesting to speak to Anthony Krause.

"Krause. May I help you?"

"Anthony. John O'Donovan here."

"Hey, old bud, what's up with the easy life?" Then he laughed hardily.

"I was reading about your story on the missing teacher. What do you know?"

"Hey John, this one is good. We cannot find a damn thing. Just like she, 'poof,' disappeared. No one saw a damn thing, and I mean nothing. The local police, well, they have nothing. But we expect that. The state is involved, and they can't turn up anything. So they have contacted the FBI, and I guess they are taking over. Other than that, well, that's it. Why? Did you know this woman?"

"Well, indirectly, I knew of her, is about it."

"Say...maybe you can help me here. What do you say?"

"No problem, if I can, I'll let you know if I hear anything," John assured Krause.

"Good, maybe we could work together on this one. You can come out of retirement." Then Anthony laughed. "No, seriously, what do you think?"

"Well, maybe. I may be able to dig up something for you to get a good headline or two. But forget the out-of-retirement. I just want a little article here and there to keep in shape. No by-lines."

"John, do you think, naaa..."

"What?" John asked.

"Well, do you remember.... I mean, I know you will remember, but anyway, a few months ago, let me think, close to a year ago, the Finkel story?"

"Yes, I remember. Why?"

"Well, do you think that...that, what was his name...ohh, you know, that teacher friend of yours you told me about, the one that had all the problems over the years. Hell, way back in the '80s and '90s. What was his name? Damn, why is it I can never remember that guy's name? Hold it. I got it here someplace in all my old notes."

John never spoke. He heard Anthony shuffling papers and talking to himself.

"Ah, yes, found it, O'Francis."

"That's it. O'Francis, yeah. Do..." John cut him off.

"No, I do not!"

"Well, I just wanted to ask...you know, a lot of talking went on back then with his name being the center of the conversation. So I just wondered if there may be some connection."

"I'll poke around, and if I dig up something, I'll call you."

As John hung up the phone, he knew that it had started. Did James Patrick have anything to do with it? That was a critical question. Was it possible that the mystery person he once inferred, whoever he was, was 'Blind Justice?' If James Patrick had made his mind up to the moral issue, the police and newspapers were in for many unsolved mystery cases.

Many questions went through John's mind for the rest of the day and evening and several libations.

An Offer

James Patrick had been a "burned out" teacher for several years, one absurd conflict after another, never seeming to let up. His thoughts turned to how Ho Chi Minh had defeated the French and the United States with staying power and constant pressure on his foe until they broke. It seemed to O'Francis that the sons of bitches in the political arena in Reynolds County had adopted "Ho's" philosophy. Instead of the lead from the end of an AK-47, something he could counter, they attacked his character, name, and family. There seemed to be no defense against this tactic.

O'Francis' will of self-discipline was once again at the very breaking point. How often would it reach that point without snapping? Like a rubber band, stretched back and forth repeatedly until it finely weakens to the point that stretching it to its maximum point, it breaks. Stress was a constant companion again, creating anxiety and chest pains frequently.

Andrew Duponte and Linnet Thomas, supervisors from the central office, had requested Jim to report to his principal's office. Over the years, he had been investigated so many times by the same two supervisors that he began to like them. Not for what they were doing so much, but because he knew they were doing what their Fuhrer told them. Good soldiers, just doing the job they were hired to do. But unfortunately, the pattern had become routine.

He could never figure out whether the two liked harassing him or if they were really just doing their job. If it was just a job, he could handle that. However, if it was the enjoyment of harassment, he had a major problem with both. That question was something he would deal with in time.

He entered Mr. Wolffe's office. Ms. Thomas was behind Wolffe's desk, and Duponte was in a chair to the left of the door. Jim smiled and placed his tape recorder down on Wolffe's desk.

"You know folks, we are really going to have to stop meeting me like this. People are beginning to talk about us."

Duponte forced a half-laugh, and Thomas just smiled. Jim took a mental note that she had a warm, genuine smile. He never figured her for the Gestapo type but felt that she most likely could be rather harsh if she needed to be. Yet, over several like meetings and investigations, there was something about her that he had noted did not fit the Marshy storm trooper mentality.

"I want to inform you two that this conference will be recorded. On 28 May 1998, present here is the good Dr. Thomas and Mr. Duponte. Both are supervisors from the Center Office staff." Jim paused momentarily.

"Now, since I only see you two here whenever someone files an observed, mendacious complaint, and I might add, brought on by some nefarious person, what have we got today?" O'Francis did not let the supervisors speak. Instead, he was irritated and lashed out with a sarcastic remark.

"Let me see. Grades! No, too much homework! No, it could not be that because I give very little of that, and we have covered all that several times. Ahh, yes, I broke up a fight the wrong way. Maybe I corrected some of my precious little students in a manner that they did not like. Or is it another child whose daddy or mommy is politically connected, and they just do not like how I am teaching? AHHH, that is it!" Jim exclaimed in excitement.

"Teaching. Now that is a real joke. That's it. I am trying to teach. Nowwww, we all know at this point that it is really not allowed in my classroom! Trying to pass along knowledge. Oh, my, out of the question!"

Both supervisors sat in silence as if O'Francis' oratory and seemingly insane statements stunned them. By all appearances, James Patrick O'Francis had finally broken. Then, finally, Duponte, in his usual deep voice, which by his appearance he would not have such, spoke.

"No, actually Mr. O'Francis, we are here today to make you an offer. There have not been any complaints." Andrew replied.

"You are kidding. No complaints. Geez, I am really in a state of total shock! Now that is a real news item. The point of fact is it should make headlines. Hell, maybe CNN! Ahh, wait. You stated you were here to make me an offer. Now that would not be an offer I cannot refuse, would it?"

Jim did not smile with his statement. Instead, he looked directly at Duponte. His eyes were filled with the emptiness of a black hole. The statement Duponte made of 'an offer he could not refuse' implied more to Jim than either one of the two could have possibly imagined.

"No, we are not kidding." Andrew laughed a true laugh, and Jim thought he would never see Duponte really have a burst of truly joyous laughter in his presence.

"Mr. O'Francis, we are here to offer you a job." Then Andrew paused for a moment waiting for a response from James P. There was none. So O'Francis sat in silence, looking at Duponte.

"Okay, ahh," Andrew continued, "We have an opening for a homebound secondary teacher. We would like for you to take it."

Again he paused and waited for Jim to say something. He did not. Jim broke his eye contact with Duponte and went to Thomas.

Several seconds of unconformable silence passed before O'Francis spoke.

"What are the requirements for doing this job?" O'Francis asked with a degree of less anxiety in his voice.

"Now, Mr. O'Francis, you are really going to like it," Andrew spoke with excitement and moved up to the edge of his chair.

"You will meet with the homebound students at their homes and make sure they get the work from their regular teachers and get it back to the students' teachers."

"Do I have to grade their work?"

Duponte looked at Thomas, and she spoke for the first time in the meeting. "No. You will not have to grade any papers," she stated firmly in a pleasant voice.

"And that is it?" Jim responded.

"Well," Andrew continued, "That is about it."

Jim sat in silence, looking at first one, then the other.

"What about a car?" O'Francis inquired.

"Well, ahh." The simple question caught Duponte off guard.

"Look, Andrew," Jim continued, "I sure will not drive my car all over the county, to whatever God-forsaken place, up some God-forsaken hollow. So you will just have to come up with one of your old best junkers for me. Now, of course," then O'Francis paused, and a smile slowly crept across his face. "If ole LaMar," Jim spoke slowly, "wants to give me one of those big fancy county 'Crown Vic' cars that you all drive all over hell and half of Georgia... Oh, I am so very sorry." Jim drew out his words as if he had just spoken a Bible belt 'go to hell' statement. "I mean Tennessee. Georgia and Alabama are not where you would find Marshy, would you?"

Andrew did not respond to O'Francis' sarcasm. He was so wrapped up in his blind devotion to LaMar that any satirical humor directed toward Marshy was considered blasphemy.

"Naaa, I did not think neither you nor good ole' LaMar would go for that. But do I get a county car?" Jim concluded with a more serious tone. Jim noticed that Thomas had broken yet another smile in his moment of humor with his peripheral vision.

"Yes, we think we can arrange that," Andrew answered.

"No, not quite yet, Mr. Duponte. You stated, I think. I would like a confirmed yes or no on my request."

Again Andrew looked over at Thomas. And for the second time, she spoke, "Yes, Mr. O'Francis, we can provide you with transportation."

"Thank you. Now, what about an office?"

"An office, well, ahh?" Andrew responded with a question in his voice.

"Yes, an office. I do not expect I will be in a car the entire year. I mean, I can do some quick calculating. I will have paperwork of some type. Where will I do this work?"

No one was talking. Jim looked over at Linnet Thomas. "Well, Dr. Thomas, do I get my own office to do my work or not?"

"Yes, I think we can provide you with an office. And Mr. O'Francis, before you say anything about '*I think,*' I have to check on a place and run it by Mr. Marshy. But I really do believe we will find you a place."

O'Francis smiled. "One more question, Dr. Thomas. Who will be my direct supervisor?"

"That would be Ms. French."

With a surprised tone in his voice, Jim responded quickly, "Rebecca Ellen French?"

"Yes. Why, is that a problem?" Andrew questioned.

"Well, Mr. Duponte, given the fact that according to my sources, she does not like me. Well, let me re-phrase that a little bit. She despises me! Yes, I would safely say that is a problem."

"Now, Mr. O'Francis. Ms. French has never said she did not like you," Andrew stated, hoping to smooth out what he knew to be true.

"Right! And I believe in the Easter bunny, Andrew! Look, I really do not care. If she can work with me, I can work with her. Adjust and overcome. I tell you what, Andrew..." Then Jim paused, his mind working rapidly to gather his thoughts before speaking.

"You ask her to come by my room Friday, and we will go over what she expects of me and how she wants the job done. Maybe we can reach some sort of compromise. Hell Andrew, who knows, we may even get to know each other to the point of understanding and liking one another. Would that not be a real ass-kick for everyone in the central office? French and O'Francis are working together, getting along, and actually like each other. Wow!"

Andrew only responded to O'Francis' request for a Friday meeting. "Okay. I don't see that as a problem. Do you, Dr. Thomas?"

"No. I really believe that you and Ms. French will work well together." Thomas stated.

"Okay, I accept the job." Jim rose, picked up his tape recorder, then thanked the two lieutenants from LaMar Marshy's headquarters and walked happily out of the office and down the long hallway to his room.

James P. spoke to himself. "Wow, new job in the fall and a new boss." I did not care anymore, just as long as he could provide for my family. The fucking title is meaningless. I figured they would force me to take the job if I refused. They have the power to do so. There is not a damn thing I can do about any transfer to wherever. It is, after all, an autocratic and oligarchical system.

Surprise Visit

I had not seen Jim in several months, so I decided to pay him a surprise visit to his school, when teachers were finishing up for the year, and there were no students, I figured I would not be disrupting anything, and we might have some time to talk. In addition, I wanted to see his junior high classroom and just get in touch with him to see how the end of the year had gone for him.

After following the proper protocol and getting directions from the assistant principal, I walked down the very long hallway to his room. His door was open, and I pecked on the side of the door. Jim looked up from what he was doing at his desk, and a smile came across his momentarily stern face.

"Oh my, come in, John. What in the world brings you to this neck of the woods?"

"Ah, I just thought I would stop by to see if you were still breathing. I have not heard from you in some time. And I wanted to see where you worked."

He rose from his chair and approached me as I walked across the room. He waved his arms open and looked around the room to indicate this was it, stating, "You have it, my little world of education."

As I surveyed the layout of his room, it was not what I expected. Instead of the usual classroom desks, he had tables with chairs at the tables. It looked more like a lunchroom setting than a classroom. But I knew that Jim was different and did not fit the round holes that most, if not all, schools, teachers, and classrooms were made up of.

"So, Jim, what is with the tables?"

"Ah, yes. The tables. I got this idea of making the setting more of a social atmosphere than the usual stressful, same ole same ole boring classroom the students have to walk into daily. So, I gathered enough unused tables and chairs to cover my usual 25 to thirty students. Hey, they liked it, and my productivity improved, in addition to the music I played for them. I did have regular desks for them; however, they were arranged in a horseshoe shape. I always hated looking at the back of a peer's head and having someone behind me and not being able to see them. Thus, the 'U' shaped arrangement.

I stood and looked at all the posters. Some commercially bought, some I could tell were hand-drawn by Jim, all with educational messages scattered about the room. In the upper right-hand corner of the chalkboard was a section blocked off with the words: Welcome to O'Francis' Think Tank. Rules:

Words you can use in the classroom: YES; NO; PLEASE; THANK YOU; MAY I. Words you cannot use in the classroom: YEAH, NAA, NOPE. Always remember, the most powerful weapon on earth is? The worst thing you can waste is?

"Interesting. One question," John asked.

"Okay, shoot," Jim stated.

"How long has the message been up in the corner?" I indicated with my head.

"All year, every year."

"I am sure they know the answer to the two questions, correct?"

"Yes. I gave them the answer on the first of the year, once. It is on every test I give. I make my own tests. No commercially "cookie-cutter" made tests in my class. Never have, never will."

"The answers are?"

At that, Jim broke out into a full-face smile. "Oh, my John. One time only. Knowledge. The mind."

"Ah, okay. One more question, if I may."

"Sure."

"How do you keep the students from looking off someone else's paper while taking a test?" Shall I use the word, cheating? Or James Patrick smiled and started walking toward his desk to the far right corner of the room, just in front of the row of windows that stretched the room's length. I followed him. He pulled out one of the chairs and placed it beside his desk as he sat in his chair.

"Have a seat, John. Now to my students cheating. Well, let me state for your record, as I know you are mentally recording all of this. I have had few students cheat in any of my classes here at the junior high level and at the high school level, where they are more brave and daring and more likely to attempt to cheat. Before you ask why, the good reporter you are, they learn quickly that they do not have to cheat to pass my classes. Together we will find a way for them to learn and pass my course if they desire to obtain knowledge and move forward in their education. First, we establish the honor system. For the most part, that has worked for me through the years. I am sure I have missed on some occasions, but I will say, 95% of the time, my students adhere to 'O's' honor system."

This was the first time I had heard him refer to himself in such a manner. Of course, I had listened to his students and ballplayers do so, but not Jim.

"I get it. Understood. I did not think anything like that existed in a public school setting."

"Can I offer you some coffee? I have my own coffee maker." Jim pointed over to a sink and a counter with a coffee maker. There were three cups upside down on the counter and a roll of paper towels.

"You are set here. You are in the same room."

"One does not have to move. Little different here than at the high school. Well, for me at any rate." He got up and made his way to the far side of the room. "Black, I still presume?"

"Yes," he stated that it was fresh, maybe an hour old, as he poured.

"So, my friend, tell me about your year as we have not seen each other in eight months."

Jim smiled. "Well, it has been interesting to say the least."

I was not sure how to take that, given the pattern of his past years. Given his nature and ideology, I automatically presumed that he had spent more time in the office than any of his students had. And given that 98% of the faculty was female, I knew he had more than any of them.

"Well, John, let me say this is my last year at this school. I have been given an 'offer I cannot refuse.' He proceeded to tell the events that had transpired throughout the last few weeks. By that time, I had retrieved my tape recorder and had placed it on the corner of his desk. He just smiled and never missed a beat in telling me what had gone down.

"I have no idea what to expect in this new position I am about to enter. But, I know one thing, I will miss the interaction with the students in the classroom. Well, for the most part."

"Bet you have had some good and interesting ones, ha."

"Well, yes, point of fact, I have."

As he looked across the empty room toward the door, we sat in silence for three minutes. Then, finally, he took a sip of his coffee and turned his head toward me.

"You see, John, when you have students like, ah, let me think for a second. Ah, José Pickens, whose mind is about three years ahead of everyone in his class, and to some extent above some of his other teachers, not too sure he was not above mine, and you can really enjoy teaching. And let me add, his sister Heather was not far behind him. José was like a giant sponge, soaking up every bit of knowledge he could about the subject matter I was presenting to him. I will tell you this, and I will predict that the high school teachers who encounter him will be challenged to keep him from being bored out of his gourd. He thinks way ahead of most everyone. But hell, he was not the only one. Shit, let me think. I have had several that just popped out at you, and you know they are special. Some in their own way, some a little on the odd side, but that does not diminish the quality of their young minds. Minds that are ahead of their ages."

He was up and across the room for a refill, then he walked to the door and closed it. As he walked back across the room in his jeans, polo shirt, and sandals, "Jesus wegons," as he always referred to them, he continued, "Echo, John. Sound travels out into the hall, and ears are attuned to anything I say, do, or company I may have. Anybody else, no one gives two fucks on a sunny Sunday afternoon!"

"I understand." With a smile on my face with his depiction of who would or would not care.

"I have a couple more days to put in and pack my shit and clear out, to the joy, I am sure, of several teachers. Well, there is one across the hall: an excellent teacher, caring, professional, that has been a great asset to me over the past several years I have been here."

"What about the current principal?"

Jim had a little chuckle before he answered.

"Well, he is all part of the establishment. I have learned part of the plan, and I might add, John, my sources are solid."

"Oh, I have no doubt," I stated.

"But here again, you see just how a negative can creep into a conversation about the joy of teaching good students and the joy I get from watching them as they absorb knowledge."

John took a drink of coffee and paused for a few seconds. "Yes, Jim, I know, and I know what you have endured over the years. But, I, well, to be honest with you, and as a 'Brother,' cannot figure out how or, for that matter, why you and Dawn stayed in this community or this county. I know— your sons. But damn, man."

Jim did not say anything for a few minutes, then he said, with a smile, as if he just thought of something pleasant. "Okay, let me take another one of my 'thinking' students. Nobel Bryan, big for his age, a gentle giant, never said spit, quiet, kind of shy, but damn, was he smart. Shit, eat you up with knowledge. Sucked it in like a vacuum cleaner. He aced 99% of all my tests. He will be another one that will challenge his high school teachers. Or, of course, be bored with their same ole same ole shit out of an ancient text and method of delivering 'knowledge' to the students.

"Now John, do not get me wrong with all my negativity about the high school teachers. A few are damn good, challenge their students, and stay on top of new educational ideals. However, I do not use the word few lightly."

"How do you remember these, well, for lack of another word at the moment, so-called standouts or extra smart ones?"

"Because that is what they are, standouts. Shit, John, there are a lot. This area is full of brilliant students who will do and be great in whatever chosen fields they settle on. I mean, you have Blake Vanpelt, who I am sure will make it in a field that will carry him far into the future. Oh, and for your record, Blake is from an area just a few miles north of this, this pious little 'village' that is viewed as lower class and ignorant. Now, he is all boy at present, but he is smart. Oh, I cannot forget Jonathan Bentley Hogg. Now you are talking about an odd duck in class. You can just tell; he will add gray to his mother's and dad's hair before it's all said and done. But, John, all that does not take away from the mind. You have students like him who, at his age, are thinking out of the box. Students like him I can relate to. You can give them so many tools to carry forward in their minds that will challenge others, including teachers, who in all likelihood will be offended by their intellect. And will not want or allow them to think out of the proverbial box, especially in such a conservative cultural area like this one. I mean, John, you still have people out in the public who think that to have any type of real discipline in the school, you have to take a goddamn piece of wood and beat the hell out of them, and then you have control. You talk about authoritarianism. Does that tell you anything? And that is technically assault and battery. I do not care what the fucked up school systems' policies are. Assault is assault. And with a weapon!"

I sat and looked at Jim to say, "*You are kidding, right?*" But I could see the expression on his face that he was not kidding at all. "So you have had a good few years?"

"Yes, for the most part. A few encounters, a few investigations."

I got up and got myself a fresh cup of coffee, which really was good coffee. I've sure had a lot worse. "May I ask why you were investigated?"

"Sure. Because I used excessive force in breaking up a fight, right there," as he pointed to the center of the room.

After asking him to elaborate on the event, he explained.

I sat and looked at him as he finished. It took me a few minutes to calibrate the aftermath of what he went through.

"Jim, I do not quite understand. What did you do wrong? I mean, what were you supposed to do?"

"I was too rough with them," Jim responded.

"That is it. Are you kidding me? I mean, is that what you were told? I mean, really?"

"Yes, John, that is exactly what I was told. That is exactly what went down, just like I have described to you."

"Well, why didn't the principal take over from the beginning when you passed him standing at that teacher's door across the hallway. He had to see you escorting the students to his office?"

"Shit!" is all Jim said, and he moved on to several other not-so-pleasant events, with the same group investigating O'Francis for what appeared to me as bullshit.

I wondered what these people would do in the large city school where I went. They would not survive more than a week, where they had real problems to contend with. Everything about James Patrick and his trials and tribulations ceased to amaze me. He had a 'target,' not just on his 'back,' his entire body was a 'target,' and one would have to be totally blind and have their head stuck in a pile of sand not to have seen it.

He told me a story about a student who was not allowed to go to the restroom, and she urinated on herself at her desk. Embarrassing to anyone, especially a girl in the seventh grade. The sad part of the story was even though the parent (a single mother) filed a complaint against the teacher, not one thing was done. No central office staff investigation. No apology. Nothing.

One point I must make in relating James P.'s life as a simple teacher, the insensitive teacher was a female.

I spent several hours with him that day, recounting the good and the not-so-good of his years on the middle school teaching level. I wondered if somebody was setting him up with his new position to fire him and how he would handle it, even if he could—knowing him as I did and knowing PTSD veterans. There was a point where everything fell apart. Usually, when that occurred, somebody got hurt.

The Narrator

I had received many phone calls from the reporters at the local newspaper, but I had nothing for them. I really did not know where James Patrick O'Francis was. I do not think that any of the reporters believed me, and I do not believe I had it in me to tell them if I did.

The investigation into the mysterious disappearance and deaths of so many people in such a small area eventually made its way to the national headlines and special interest stories. However, with all the sources the law enforcement and the news media and newspapers had, no one could pinpoint anyone behind what seemed to be a string of mysterious deaths and disappearances.

James Patrick's name soon faded into the mysteries along with missing or dead.

I often sat on my deck on my mountain top in my little isolated world with Boaz close by or on my lap, and when the late afternoon sun drifts slowly down into the west, I think about the not so simple teacher I had gotten to know. As a journalist, you develop a certain instinct over the years, and I knew that he was not dead. Missing, perhaps, from whom he wanted to be missing. Often my thoughts turn to how he was doing and if he had a forest to go walking.

James Patrick had gotten me into the habit of walking and thinking and had taught me to listen to the forest and all the animals seen as well as unseen. I continue to go for my early evening strolls along the same paths he and I once walked. I never did create any new ones in the additional acres I had obtained. I could only hope that he had found the peace he had been searching for.

He was a man of his word. I have given a lot of thought to this man and his philosophy and concluded that those whose words are void of honor and integrity and are filled with mendacity, their actions shrouded in deceit, should never test such men as James Patrick O'Francis.

There is no time limit for such people, and the ultimate consequences can only result in their loss. I wonder how long it would go on. How many would he feel was enough before justice was reached?

Forever and a day, her presence is always felt.

Christine J.